Marx Joyce
Hardy Austen
Defoe Abbott Hugo
Melville Emerson Eliot
Montaigne Chesterton Cooper Grimm
Machiavelli
Stoker Haggard Molière
Wilde Carroll Christie Byron Schiller
Maupassant Engels
Garnett Einstein Fitzgerald Hawthorne Smith Kafka
Goethe Dostoyevsky Hall
Cotton Kipling Doyle Willis
Baum Henry Nietzsche
Leslie Dumas Flaubert Turgenev Balzac
Stockton Vatsyayana Crane
Burroughs Verne
Curtis Tocqueville Gogol Vinci
Homer Widger Tolstoy Whitman Busch
Darwin Thoreau
Potter Freud Zola Twain Scott
Kant Jowett Stevenson Dickens Plato Harte
Lawrence Burton Hesse
Andersen
London Descartes Cervantes
Poe Aristotle Wells Voltaire Cooke
Hale James Hastings Irving
Bunner Shakespeare
Richter Chambers
Doré Dante Chekhov Shaw Benedict Alcott
Swift da Wodehouse Pushkin
Newton

tredition

tredition was established in 2006 by Sandra Latusseck and Soenke Schulz. Based in Hamburg, Germany, tredition offers publishing solutions to authors and publishing houses, combined with world-wide distribution of printed and digital book content. tredition is uniquely positioned to enable authors and publishing houses to create books on their own terms and without conventional manu-facturing risks.

For more information please visit: www.tredition.com

TREDITION CLASSICS

This book is part of the TREDITION CLASSICS series. The creators of this series are united by passion for literature and driven by the intention of making all public domain books available in printed format again - worldwide. Most TREDITION CLASSICS titles have been out of print and off the bookstore shelves for decades. At tredition we believe that a great book never goes out of style and that its value is eternal. Several mostly non-profit literature projects provide content to tredition. To support their good work, tredition donates a portion of the proceeds from each sold copy. As a reader of a TREDITION CLASSICS book, you support our mission to save many of the amazing works of world literature from oblivion. See all available books at www.tredition.com.

Project Gutenberg

The content for this book has been graciously provided by Project Gutenberg. Project Gutenberg is a non-profit organization founded by Michael Hart in 1971 at the University of Illinois. The mission of Project Gutenberg is simple: To encourage the creation and distribution of eBooks. Project Gutenberg is the first and largest collection of public domain eBooks.

The Ethics of George Eliot's Works

John Crombie Brown

Imprint

This book is part of TREDITION CLASSICS

Author: John Crombie Brown
Cover design: Buchgut, Berlin – Germany

Publisher: tredition GmbH, Hamburg - Germany
ISBN: 978-3-8424-8346-0

www.tredition.com
www.tredition.de

PREFACE.

The greater part of the following Essay was written several years ago. It was too long for any of the periodicals to which the author had been in the habit of occasionally contributing, and no thought was then entertained of publishing it in a separate form. One day, however, during his last illness, the talk happened to turn on George Eliot's Works, and he mentioned his long-forgotten paper. One of the friends then present—a competent critic and high literary authority—expressed a wish to see it, and his opinion was so favourable that its publication was determined on. The author then proposed to complete his work by taking p. viup 'Middlemarch' and 'Deronda'; and if any trace of failing vigour is discernible in these latter pages, the reader will bear in mind that the greater portion of them was composed when the author was rapidly sinking under a painful disease, and that the concluding paragraphs were dictated to his daughter after the power of writing had failed him, only five days before his death.

PREFACE TO THIRD EDITION.

It is a source of great gratification to the friends of the author that his little volume has already been so well received that the second edition has been out of print for some time. In now publishing a third, they have been influenced by two considerations,—the continued demand for the book, and the favourable opinion expressed of it by "George Eliot" herself, which, since her lamented death, delicacy no longer forbids them to make public.

In a letter to her friend and publisher, the late Mr John Blackwood, received soon after the appearance of the first edition, she writes, with reference to certain passages: "They seemed to me more penetrating and finely felt than almost anything I have read in the way of printed comments on my own writings." Again, in a letter to a friend of the author, p. viiishe says: "When I read the volume in the summer, I felt as if I had been deprived of something that should have fallen to my share in never having made his personal acquaintance. And it would have been a great benefit,—a great stimulus to me to have known some years earlier that my work was being sanctioned by the sympathy of a mind endowed with so much insight and delicate sensibility. It is difficult for me to speak of what others may regard as an excessive estimate of my own work, but I will venture to mention the keen perception shown in the note on page 29, as something that gave me peculiar satisfaction."

Once more. In an article in the 'Contemporary Review' of last month, on "The Moral Influence of George Eliot," by "One who knew her," the writer says: "It happens that the only criticism which we have heard mentioned as giving her pleasure, was a little posthumous volume published by Messrs Blackwood."

With such testimony in its favour, it is hoped a third edition will not be thought uncalled for.

March 1881.

THE ETHICS OF GEORGE ELIOT'S WORKS.

"There is in man a higher than love of happiness: he can do without happiness, and instead thereof find blessedness."

Such may be regarded as the fundamental lesson which one of the great teachers of our time has been labouring to impress upon the age. The truth, and the practical corollary from it, are not now first enunciated. Representing, as we believe it to do, the practical aspect of the noblest reality in man—that which most directly represents Him in whose image he is made—it has found doctrinal expression more or less perfect from the earliest times. The older Theosophies and Philosophies—Gymnosophist and Cynic, Chaldaic and Pythagorean, Epicurean and Stoic, Platonist and Eclectic—were all attempts to embody it in teaching, and to carry it out in life. p. 2They saw, indeed, but imperfectly, and their expressions of the truth are all one-sided and inadequate. But they did see, in direct antagonism alike to the popular view and to the natural instinct of the animal man, that what is ordinarily called happiness does not represent the highest capability in humanity, or meet its indefinite aspirations; and that in degree as it is consciously made so, life becomes animalised and degraded. The whole scheme of Judaism, as first promulgated in all the stern simplicity of its awful Theism, where the Divine is fundamentally and emphatically represented as the Omnipotent and the Avenger, was an emphatic protest against that self-isolation in which the man folds himself up like a chrysalid in its cocoon whenever his individual happiness—the so-called saving of his own soul—becomes the aim and aspiration of his life. In one sense the Jew of Moses had no individual as apart from a national existence. The secret sin of Achan, the vaunting pride of David, call forth less individual than national calamity.

At last in the fulness of time there came forth One—whence and how we do not stop to inquire—who gathered up into Himself all these tangled, broken, often divergent threads; who gave to this truth, so far as one very brief human life could give—at once its perfect and exhaustive doctrinal expression, and its essentially perfect and exhaustive practical exemplification, by life and by death. Endless controversies p. 3have stormed and are still storming around that name which He so significantly and emphatically appropriated — the "Son of Man." But from amid all the controversy that veils it, one fact, clear, sharp, and unchallenged, stands out as the very life and seal of His human greatness — "He pleased not Himself." By every act He did, every word He spoke, and every pain He bore, He put away from Him happiness as the aim and end of man. He reduced it to its true position of a possible accessory and issue of man's highest fulfilment of life — an issue, the contemplation of which might be of some avail as the being first awoke to its nobler capabilities, but which, the more the life went on towards realisation, passed the more away from conscious regard.

Thenceforth the Cross, as the typical representation of this truth, became a recognised power on the earth. Thenceforth every great teacher of humanity within the pale of nominal Christendom, whatever his apparent tenets or formal creed, has been, in degree as he was great and true, explicitly or implicitly the expounder of this truth; every great and worthy life, in degree as it assimilated to that ideal life, has been the practical embodiment of it. "Endure hardness," said one of its greatest apostles and martyrs, "as good soldiers of Christ." And to the endurance of hardness; to the recognition of something in humanity to which what we ordinarily call life and all its joys are of no account; to the abnegation p. 4of mere happiness as aim or end, — to this the world of Christendom thenceforth became pledged, if it would not deny its Head and trample on His cross.

In no age has the truth been a popular one: when it becomes so, the triumph of the Cross — and in it the practical redemption of humanity — will be near at hand. Yet in no age — not the darkest and most corrupt Christendom has yet seen — have God and His Christ been without their witnesses to the higher truth, — witnesses, if not by speech and doctrine, yet by life and death. Even monasticism, harshly as we may now judge it, arose, in part at least, through the desire to "endure hardness;" only it turned aside from the hardness appointed in the world without, to choose, and ere long to make, a hardness of its own; and then, self-seeking, and therefore anti-Christian, it fell. Amid all its actual corruption the Church stands forth a living witness, by its ritual and its sacraments, to this fundamental truth of the Cross; and ever and anon from its deepest degradation there emerges clear and sharp some figure bending under this noblest burden of our doom—some Savonarola or St Francis charged with the one thought of truth and right, of the highest truth and right, to be followed, if need were, through the darkness of death and of hell.

Perhaps few ages have needed more than our own to have this fundamental principle of Christian ethics—this doctrine of the Cross—sharply and strongly p. 5proclaimed to it. Our vast advances in physical science tend, in the first instance at least, to withdraw regard from the higher requirements of life. Even the progress of commerce and navigation, at once multiplying the means and extending the sphere of physical and fsthetic enjoyment, aids to intensify the appetite for these. Systems of so-called philosophy start undoubtingly with the axiom that happiness is the one aim of man: and with at least some of these happiness is simply coincident with physical well-being. Political Economy aims as undoubtingly to act on the principle, "the greatest possible happiness of the greatest possible number:" and perhaps, as Political Economy claims to deal with man in his physical life only, it were unreasonable to expect from it regard to aught above this. Our current and popular literature—Fiction, Poetry, Essays on social relations—is emphatically a literature of enjoyment, ministering to the various excitements of pleasure, wonder, suspense, or pain. And last, and in some respects most serious of all, our popular theology has largely conformed to the spirit of the age. Representative of a debased and emasculated Christianity, it attacks our humanity at its very core. It rings out to us, with wearisome iteration, as our one great concern, the saving of our own souls: degrades the religion of the Cross into a slightly-refined and long-sighted selfishness: and makes our following Him who "pleased not Himself" to consist in doing just enough to p. 6escape what it calls the pains of hell—to win what it calls the joys of heaven.

This is the dark side of the picture; but it has its bright side too. These advances of science, these extensions of commerce, these philosophies, even where they are falsely so called, this Political Economy, which from its very nature must first "labour for the meat that perisheth,"—these are all God's servants and man's ministers still—the ministers of man's higher and nobler life. Consciously or unconsciously, they are working to raise from myriads burdens of poverty, care, ceaseless and fruitless toil, under the pressure of which all higher aspiration is wellnigh impossible. Sanitary reform in itself may mean nothing more than better drainage, fresher air, freer light, more abundant water: to the "Governor among the nations" it means lessened impossibility that men should live to Him.

If in few ages the great bulk and the most popular portion of literature has more prostituted itself to purposes of sensational or at most fsthetic enjoyment, it is at least as doubtful if in any previous age our highest literature has more emphatically and persistently devoted itself to proclaiming this great doctrine of the Cross. Sometimes directly and explicitly, oftener by implication, this is the ultimate theme of those who are most deeply influencing the spirit of the time. Our finest and most widely recognised pulpit oratory is at home here, and only here: p. 7Maurice and Arnold, Trench and Vaughan, Robertson and Stanley, James Martineau and Seeley, Thirlwall and Wilberforce, Kingsley and Brooke, Caird and Tulloch, different in form, in much antagonistic in what is called opinion, are of one mind and heart on this. The thought underlying all their thoughts of man is that "higher than love of happiness" in humanity which expresses the true link between man and God. The practical doctrine that with them underlies all others is, "Love not pleasure — love God. Love Him not alone in the light and amid the calm, but through the blackness and the storm. Though He hide Himself in the thick darkness, yet" give thanks at remembrance of His holiness. "Though He slay thee, yet trust still in Him." The hope to which they call us is not, save secondarily and incidentally, the hope of a great exhaustless future. It is the hope of a true life *now*, struggling on and up through hardness and toil and battle, careless though its crown be the crown of thorns.

Even evangelicism indirectly, in great degree unconsciously, bears witness to the truth through its demand of absolute self-abnegation before God: though the inversion of the very idea of Him fundamentally involved in its scheme makes the self-abnegation no longer that of the son, but of the slave; includes in it the denial of that law which Himself has written on our hearts; and would substitute our subjection to an arbitrary despotism for our being p. 8"made partakers of His holiness." One of the sternest and most consistent of Calvinistic theologians, Jonathan Edwards, in one of his works expresses his willingness to be damned for the glory of God, and to rejoice in his own damnation: with a strange, almost incredible, obliquity of moral and spiritual insight failing to perceive that in thus losing himself in the infinite of holy Love lies the very essence of human blessedness, that this and this alone is in very truth his "eternal life."

Among what may be called Essayists, two by general consent stand out as most deeply penetrating and informing the spirit of the age — Carlyle and Ruskin. To the former, brief reference has already been made. In the work then quoted from, one truth has prominence above all others: that with the will's acceptance of happiness as the aim of life begins the true degradation of humanity; and that then alone true life dawns upon man when truth and right begin to stand out as the first objects of his regard. Never since has Carlyle's strong rough grasp relaxed its hold of this truth; and howsoever in later works, in what are intended as biographical illustrations of it, he may seem to confuse mere strength and energy with righteousness of will, and thence to confound outward and visible success with vital achievement, that strength and energy are always in his eyes, fighting or enduring against some phase of the many-headed hydra of wrong.

p. 9Of Ruskin it seems almost superfluous to speak. They have read him to little purpose who have not felt that all his essays and criticisms in art, all his expositions in social and political science, are essentially unified by one animating and pervading truth: the truth that to man's moral relations, or, in other words, the developing and perfecting in him of that Divine image in which he is made, — all things else, joy, beauty, life itself, are of account only to the degree in which they are consciously used to subserve that higher life. His ultimate standard of value to which everything, alike in art and in social and political relations, is referred, is — not success, not enjoyment, whether sensuous, sentimental, or fsthetic, but — the measure in which may thereby be trained up that higher life of humanity. Art is to him God's minister, not when she is simply true to nature, but solely when true to nature in such forms and phases as shall tend to bring man nearer to moral truth, beauty, and purity. The Ios and Ariadnes of the debased Italian schools, the boors of

Teniers, the Madonnas of Guido, are truer to one phase of nature than are Fra Angelico's angels, or Tintoret's Crucifixion. But that nature is humanity as degraded by sense; and therefore the measure of their truthfulness is for him also the measure of their debasement.

In poetry, the key-note so firmly struck by Wordsworth in his noble "Ode to Duty" has been as firmly and more delicately caught up by other singers; who, p. 10moreover, have seen more clearly than Wordsworth did, that it is for faith, not for sight, that duty wears

> "The Godhead's most benignant grace;"

for the path along which she leads is inevitably on earth steep, rugged, and toilsome. Take almost any one of Tennyson's more serious poems, and it will be found pervaded by the thought of life as to be fulfilled and perfected only through moral endurance and struggle. "Ulysses" is no restless aimless wanderer; he is driven forth from inaction and security by that necessity which impels the higher life, once begun within, to press on toward its perfecting this all-possible sorrow, peril, and fear. "The Lotos-eaters" are no mere legendary myth: they shadow forth what the lower instincts of our humanity are ever urging us all to seek—ease and release from the ceaseless struggle against wrong, the ceaseless straining on toward right. "In Memoriam" is the record of love "making perfect through suffering:" struggling on through the valley of the shadow of death toward the far-off, faith-seen light "behind the veil." "The Vision of Sin" portrays to us humanity choosing enjoyment as its only aim; and of necessity sinking into degradation so profound, that even the large heart and clear eye of the poet can but breathe out in sad bewilderment, "Is there any hope?"—can but dimly see, far off over the darkness, "God make Himself an awful rose of dawn." In one of the most profound of all His creationsp. 11—"The Palace of Art"—we have presented to us the soul surrounding itself with everything fair and glad, and in itself pure, not primarily to the eye, but to the mind: attempting to achieve its destiny and to fulfil its life in the perfections of intellectual beauty and fsthetic delight. But the palace of art, *made the palace of the soul*, becomes its dungeon-house, self-generating and filling fast with all loathsome and deathly shapes; and the heaven of intellectual joy becomes at last a more penetrative and intenser hell. The "Idylls of the King" are but exquisite variations on the one note—that the only true and high life of humanity is the life of full and free obedience; and that such life on earth becomes of necessity one of struggle, sorrow, outward loss and apparent failure. In "Vivien"—the most remarkable of them all for the subtlety of its conception and the delicacy of its execution,—the picture is perhaps the darkest and saddest time can show—that of a nature rich to the utmost in all lower wisdom of the mind, struggling long and apparently truly against the flesh, yet all the while dallying with the foul temptation, till the flesh prevails; and in a moment, swift and sure as the lightning, moral and spiritual death swoops down, and we see the lost one no more.

Many other illustrations might be given from our noblest and truest poetry—from the works of the Brownings, the "Saints' Tragedy" of Charles Kingsley, the dramatic poems of Henry Taylor—of the p. 12extent to which it is vitally, even where not formally Christian; the extent to which the truth of the Cross has transfused it, and become one chief source of its depth and power. But we must hasten on to our more immediate object in these remarks.

Those who read works of fiction merely for amusement, may be surprised that it should be thought possible they could be vehicles for conveying to us the deepest practical truth of Christianity,—that the highest life of man only begins when he begins to accept and to bear the Cross; and that the conscious pursuit of happiness as his highest aim tends inevitably to degrade and enslave him. Even those who read novels more thoughtfully, who recognise in them a great moral force acting for good or evil on the age, may be startled to find George Eliot put forward as the representative of this higher-toned fiction, and as entitled to take place beside any of those we have named for the depth and force, the consistency and persistence, with which she has laboured to set before us the Christian, and therefore the only exhaustively true, ideal of life.

Yet a careful examination will, we are satisfied, show that from her first appearance before the public, this thought, and the specific purpose of this teaching, have never been absent from the writer's mind; that it may be defined as the central aim of all her works: and that it gathers in force, condensation, and power throughout the series. Other qualities George Eliot p. 13has, that would of themselves entitle her to a very high place among the teachers of the time. In largeness of Christian charity, in breadth of human sympathy, in tenderness toward all human frailty that is not vitally base and self-seeking, in subtle power of finding "a soul of goodness even in things apparently evil," she has not many equals, certainly no superior, among the writers of the day. Throughout all her works we shall look in vain for one trace of the fierce self-opinionative arrogance of Carlyle, or the narrow dogmatic intolerance of Ruskin: though we shall look as vainly for one word or sign that shall, on the mere ground of intellectual power, energy, and ultimate success, condone the unprincipled ambition of a Frederick, so-called the Great, and exalt him into a hero; or find in the cold heart and mean sordid soul of a Turner an ideal, because one of those strange physiological freaks that now and then startle the world, the artist's temperament and artist's skill, were his beyond those of any man of his age. But as our object here is to attempt placing her before the reader as asserting and illustrating the highest life of humanity, as a true preacher of the doctrine of the Cross, even when least formally so, we leave these features, as well as her position as an artist, untouched on, the rather that they have all been already discussed by previous critics.

The 'Scenes of Clerical Life,' delicately outlined as they are, still profess to be but sketches. In them, p. 14however, what we have assumed to be the great moral aim of the writer comes distinctly out; and even within the series itself gathers in clearness and power. Self-sacrifice as the Divine law of life, and its only true fulfilment; self-sacrifice, not in some ideal sphere sought out for ourselves in the vain spirit of self-pleasing, but wherever God has placed us, amid homely, petty anxieties, loves, and sorrows; the aiming at the highest attainable good in our own place, irrespective of all results of joy or sorrow, of apparent success or failure,—such is the lesson that begins to be conveyed to us in these "Scenes."

The lesson comes to us in the quiet unselfish love, the sweet hourly self-devotion of the "Milly" of Amos Barton, so touchingly free and full that it never recognises itself as self-devotion at all. In "Mr Gilfil's Love-Story" we have it taught affirmatively through the deep unselfishness of Mr Gilfil's love to Tina, and his willingness to offer up even this, the one hope and joy of his life, upon the altar of duty; negatively, through the hard, cold, callous, self-pleasing of Captain Wybrow—a type of character which, never repeated, is reproduced with endless variations and modifications in nearly all the author's subsequent works. It is, however, in "Janet's Repentance" that the power of the author is put most strongly forth, and also that what we conceive to be the vital aim of her works is most definitely and firmly pronounced. Here also we have illustrated that breadth of nature, p. 15that power of discerning the true and good under whatsoever external form it may wear, which is almost a necessary adjunct of the author's true and large ideal of the Christian life. She goes, it might almost seem, out of her way to select, from that theological school with which her whole nature is most entirely at dissonance, one of her most touching illustrations of a life struggling on towards its highest through contempt, sorrow, and death. That narrowest of all sectarianisms, which arrogates to itself the name Evangelical, and which holds up as the first aim to every man the saving of his own individual soul, has furnished to her Mr Tryan, whose life is based on the principle laid down by the one great Evangelist, "He that loveth his soul shall lose it; he that hateth his soul shall keep it unto life eternal." {15}

Mr Tryan, as first represented to us, is not an engaging figure. Narrow and sectarian, full of many uncharities, to a great extent vain and self-conscious, glad to be flattered and idolised by men and women by no means of large calibre or lofty standard—it might well seem impossible to invest such a figure with one heroic element. Yet it is before this man p. 16we are constrained to bow down in reverence, as before one truer, greater, nobler than ourselves; and as we stand with Janet Dempster beside the closing grave, we may well feel that one is gone from among us whose mere presence made it less hard to fight our battle against "the world, the flesh, and the devil." The explanation of the paradox is not far to seek. The principle which animated the life now withdrawn from sight—which raised it above all its littlenesses and made it a witness for God and His Christ, constraining even the scoffers to feel the presence of "Him who is invisible"—this principle was self-sacrifice. So at least the imperfections of human speech lead us to call that which stands in antagonism to self-pleasing; but before Him to whom all things are open, what we so call is the purification and exaltation of that self in us which is the highest created reflex of His image — the growing up of it into His likeness for ever.

We may here, once for all, and very briefly, advert to one specialty of the author's works, which, if we are right in our interpretation of their central moral import, flows almost necessarily as a corollary from it. In each of these sketches one principal figure is blotted out just when our regards are fixed most strongly on it. Milly, Tina, and Mr Tryan all die, at what may well appear the crisis of life and destiny for themselves or others. There is in this — if not in specific intention, certainly in practical teaching — p. 17something deeper and more earnest than any mere artistic trick of pathos — far more real than the weary commonplace of suggesting to us any so-called immortality as the completion and elucidation of earthly life; far profounder and simpler, too, than the only less trite commonplace of hinting to us the mystery of God's ways in what we call untimely death. The true import of it we take to be the separation of all the world calls success or reward from the life that is thus seeking its highest fulfilment. In conformity with the average doctrine of "compensation," Amos Barton should have appeared before us at last installed in a comfortable living, much respected by his flock, and on good terms with his brethren and well-to-do neighbours around. With a truer and deeper wisdom, the author places him before us in that brief after-glimpse still a poor, care-worn, boweddown man, and the sweet daughter-face by his side shows the premature lines of anxiety and sorrow. Love, anguish, and death, working their true fruits within, bring no success or achievement that the eye can note. By all the principles of "poetic justice," Mr Tryan ought to have recovered and married Janet; under the influence of her larger nature to have shaken off his narrownesses; to have lived down all contempt and opposition, and become the respected influential incumbent of the town; and in due time to have toned down from his "enthusiasm of humanity" into the simply earnest, hard-working, and rather p. 18commonplace town rector. Better, because truer, as it is. Only in the earlier dawn of this higher life of the soul, either in the race or in the individual man; only in the days of the Isaacs and Jacobs of our young humanity, though not with the Abrahams, the Moses', or the Joshuas even then; only when the soul first begins to apprehend that its true relation to God is to be realised only through the Cross—is there conscience and habitual "respect unto the recompense" of *any* reward.

In 'Adam Bede,' the first of George Eliot's more elaborate works, the illustrations of the great moral purpose we have assigned to her are so numerous and varied, that it is not easy to select from among them. On the one hand, Dinah Morris—one of the most exquisitely serene and beautiful creations of fiction—and Seth and Adam Bede present to us, variously modified, the aspect of that life which is aiming toward the highest good. On the other hand, Arthur Donnithorne and Hetty Sorrel—poor little vain and shallow-hearted Hetty—bring before us the meanness, the debasement, and, if unarrested, the spiritual and remediless death inevitably associated with and accruing from that "self-pleasing" which, under one form or other, is the essence of all evil and sin. Of these, Arthur Donnithorne and Adam Bede seem to us the two who are most sharply and subtilely contrasted; and to these we shall confine our remarks.

p. 19In Arthur Donnithorne, the slight sketch placed before us in Captain Wybrow is elaborated into minute completeness, and at the same time freed from all that made Wybrow even superficially repellent. Handsome, accomplished, and gentlemanly; loving and lovable; finding his keenest enjoyment in the enjoyment of others; irreproachable in life, and free from everything bearing the semblance of vice,—what more could the most exacting fictionist desire to make up his ideal hero? Yet, without ceasing to be all thus portrayed, he scatters desolation and crime in his path. He does this, not through any revulsion of being in himself, but in virtue of that very principle of action from which his lovableness proceeds. Of duty simply as duty, of right solely as right, his knowledge is yet to come. Essentially, his ideal of life as yet is "self-pleasing." This impels him, constituted as he is, to strive that he shall stand well with all. This almost necessitates that he shall be kindly, genial, loving; enjoying the joy and well-being of all around him, and therefore lovable. But this also assures that his struggle against temptation shall be weak and vacillating; and that when, through his paltering with it, it culminates, he shall at once fall before it. The wood scene with Adam Bede still further illustrates the same characteristics. This man, so genial and kindly, rages fiercely in his heart against him whom he has unwittingly wronged. Frank and open, apparently the very soul of honour, he shuffles p. 20and lies like a coward and a knave; and this in no personal fear, but because he shrinks to lose utterly that goodwill and esteem of others, — of Adam in particular, because Adam constrains his own high esteem, — which are to him the reflection of his own self-worship. Repentance comes to him at last, because conscience has never in him been entirely overlaid and crushed. It comes when the whirlwind of anguish has swept over him, scattered all the flimsy mists of self-excuse in which self-love had sought to veil his wrong-doing, and bowed him to the dust; but who shall estimate the remediless and everlasting loss already sustained?

We have spoken of Captain Wybrow as the prototype of Arthur. He is so in respect of both being swayed by that vital sin of self-pleasing to which all wrong-doing ultimately refers itself; but that in Arthur the corruption of life at its source is not complete, is shown throughout the whole story. The very form of action which self-love assumes in him, tells that self though dominant is not yet supreme. It refers itself to others. It absolutely requires human sympathy. So long as the man lives to some extent in the opinion and affections of his brother men, — so long as he is even uncomfortable under the sense of being shut out from these otherwise than as the being so shall affect his own *interests*, — we may be quite sure he is not wholly lost. The difference between the two men is still more clearly shown when they are brought face to face with the result of their p. 21wrong-doing. With each there is sorrow, but in Wybrow, and still more vividly as we shall see in Tito Melema, it is the sorrow of self-worship only. No thought of the wronged one otherwise than as an obstacle and embarrassment, no thought of the wrong simply as a wrong, can touch him. This sorrow is merely remorse, "the sorrow of the world which worketh death." Arthur, too, is suddenly called to confront the misery and ruin he has wrought; but in him, self then loses its ascendancy. There is no attempt to plead that he was the tempted as much as the tempter; and no care now as to what others shall think or say about him. All thought is for the wretched Hetty; and all energy is concentrated on the one present object, of arresting so far as it can be arrested the irremediable loss to her. The wrong stands up before him in its own nakedness as a wrong. This is repentance; and with repentance restoration becomes possible and begins.

Adam Bede contrasts at nearly every point with Arthur Donnithorne. Lovable is nearly the last epithet we think of applying to him. Hard almost to cruelty toward his sinning father; hard almost to contemptuousness toward his fond, foolish mother; bitterly hard toward his young master and friend, on the first suspicion of personal wrong; savagely vindictive, long and fiercely unforgiving, when he knows that wrong accomplished;—these may well seem things irreconcilable with any true fulfilment of that Christian p. 22life whose great law is love. Yet, examined more narrowly, they approve themselves as nearly associated with the larger fulness of that life. They are born of the same spirit which said of old, "Woe unto you, Scribes and Pharisees, hypocrites!" fulfilments, howsoever imperfect, of that true and deep "law of resentment" which modern sentimentalism has all but expunged from the Christian code. The hardness is essentially against the wrong-doing, not against the doer of it; and against it rather as it affects others than as it burdens, worries, or overshadows his own life. It subsists in and springs from the intensity with which, in a nature robust and energetic in no ordinary degree, right and wrong have asserted themselves as the realities of existence. Even Seth can be more tolerant than Adam, because the gentle, placid moral beauty of his nature is, so far as this may ever be, the result of temperament; while in Adam whatever has been attained has been won through inward struggle and self-conquest.

In the 'Mill on the Floss,' the moral interest of the whole drama is concentrated to a very great degree on Maggie Tulliver; and in her is also mainly concentrated the representative struggle between good and evil, the spirit of the Cross and that of the world; for Stephen Guest is little more than the objective form under which the latent evil of her own humanity assails her. Her life is the field upon which we see the great conflict waging between the elements p. 23of spiritual life and spiritual death; swaying amid heart-struggle and pain, now toward victory, now toward defeat, till at last all seems lost. Then at one rebound the strong brave spirit recovers itself, and takes up the full burden of its cross; sees and accepts the present right though the heart is breaking; and the end is victory crowned and sealed by death.

From her first appearance as a child, those elements of humanity are most prominent in her which, unguided and uncontrolled, are most fraught with danger to the higher life; and for her there is no real outward guidance or control whatever. The passionate craving for human sympathy and love, which meets no fuller response than from the rude instinctive fondness of her father and the carefully-regulated affection of her brother, on the one hand prepares her for the storm of passion, and on the other, chilled and thrown back by neglect and refusal, threatens her with equal danger of hardness and self-inclusion. The strong artist temperament, the power of spontaneous and intense enjoyment in everything fair and glad to eye and ear, repressed by the uncongenial accessories around her, tends to concentrate her existence in a realm of mere imaginative life, where, if it be the only life, the diviner part of our being can find no sustenance. This danger is for her the greater and more insidious, because in her the sensuous, so strongly developed, is refined from p. 24all its grossness by the presence of imagination and thought.

When at last, amid the desolation that has come upon her home, and the increasing bareness of all the accessories of her young life, its deeper needs and higher aspirations awaken to definite purpose and seek definite action, the direction they take is toward a hard stern asceticism, cramping up all life and energy within a narrow round of drudgeries and privations. She strives, as many an earnest impassioned nature like hers has done in similar circumstances, to fashion her own cross, and to make it as hard as may be to bear. She would deny to herself the very beauty of earth and sky, the music of birds and rippling waters, and everything sweet and glad, as temptations and snares. From all this she is brought back by Philip. But he, touching as he is in the humility and tender unselfishness of his love, is too exclusively of the artist temperament to give direction or sustainment to the deeper moral requirements of her being. He may win her back to the love of beauty and the sense of joy; but he is not the one to stand by her side when the stern conflict between pleasure and right, sense and soul, the world and God, is being fought out within her.

With her introduction to Stephen Guest, that conflict assumes specific and tangible form; and it has emphatically to be fought out *alone*. All external circumstances are against her; even Lucy's sweet p. 25unjealous temper, and Tom's bitter hatred, combining with Philip's painful self-consciousness to keep the safeguard of his presence less constantly at her side. At last the crowning temptation comes. Without design, by a surprise on the part of both, the step has been taken which may well seem irretraceable. Going back from it is not merely going back from joy and hope, but going back to deeper loneliness than she has ever known; and going back also to misunderstanding, shame, and lifelong repentance. But conscience, the imperative requirements of the higher life within, have resumed their power. There is no paltering with that inward voice; no possibility but the acceptance of the present urgent right, — the instant fleeing from the wrong, though with it is bound up all of enjoyment life can know. It is thus she has to take up her cross, not the less hard to bear that her own hands have so far fashioned it.

One grave criticism on the death-scene has been made, that at first sight seems unanswerable. It is said that no such full, swift recognition between the brother and sister, in those last moments of their long-severed lives, is possible; because there is no true point of contact through which such recognition, on the brother's part, could ensue. We think, however, there is something revealed to us in the brother which brings him nearer to what is noblest and deepest in the sister than at first appears. He also has his ideal of duty and right: it may not be a very p. 26broad or high one, but it is there; it is something without and above mere self; and it is resolutely adhered to at whatsoever cost of personal ease or pleasure. That such aim cannot be so followed on without, to some extent, ennobling the whole nature, is shown in his love for Lucy. It has come on him, and grown up with him, unconsciously, when there was no wrong connected with it; but with her engagement to Stephen all this is changed. Hard and stern as he is to others, he is thenceforth the harder and sterner still to self. There is no paltering with temptation, such as brings the sister so near to hopeless fall. Here the cold harsh brother rises to true nobility, and shows that upon him too life has established its higher claim than that of mere self-seeking enjoyment. There is, then, this point of contact between these two, that each has an ideal of duty and light, and to it each is content to sacrifice all things else. Through this, in that death-look, they recognise each other; and the author's motto in its full significance is justified, "In their death they were not divided."

'Silas Marner,' though carefully finished, is of slighter character than any of the author's later works, and does not require lengthened notice. In Godfrey Cass we have again, though largely modified, the type of character in which self is the main object of regard, and in which, therefore, with much that is likeable, and even, for the circumstances in which it has grown p. 27up, estimable, there is little depth, truth, or steadfastness. Repentance, and, so far as it is possible, restoration, come to him mainly through the silent ministration of a purer and better nature than his own: but the self-pleasing of the past has brought about that which no repentance can fully reverse or restore. Even on the surface this is shown; for Eppie, unowned and neglected, can never become his daughter. But—far beyond and beneath this—we have here, and elsewhere throughout the author's works, indicated to us one of the most solemn, and, at the same time, most certain truths of our existence: that there are forms of accepted and fostered evil so vital that no repentance can fully blot them out from the present or the future of life. No turning away from the accursed thing, no discipline, no futurity near or far, can ever place Arthur Donnithorne or Godfrey Cass alongside Dinah Morris or Adam Bede. Their irreversible part of self-worship precludes them, by the very laws of our being, from the highest and broadest achievement of life and destiny.

Leaving for the present 'Romola,' as in many respects more directly linking itself with George Eliot's great poetic effort, 'The Spanish Gypsy,' we turn for a little to 'Felix Holt,' the next of her English tales. It would be perhaps natural to select, from among the characters here presented to us, in illustration of life consciously attuning itself to the highest aim irrespective of any end save that aim itself, one or other of p. 28the two in whom this is most palpably presented to us—Felix himself or Esther Lyon. We prefer, however, selecting Harold Transome, certainly one of the most difficult and one of the most strikingly wrought out conceptions, not only in the works of George Eliot, but in modern fiction.

Harold, we believe, is not a general favourite with the modern public, any more than he was with his own contemporaries. He has none of those lovablenesses which make Arthur Donnithorne so attractive; and at first sight nothing of that uncompromising sense of right which characterises Adam Bede. He comes before us apparently no more than a clearheaded, hard, shrewd, successful man of the world, greatly alive to his own interests and importance, and with no particular principles to boast of.

How does it come that this man, when over and over again, in great things and in small, two paths lie before him to choose, always chooses the truer and better of the two? When Felix attempts to interfere in the conduct of his election, even while resenting the interference as impertinent, he sets himself honestly to attempt to arrest the wrong. He buys Christian's secret; but it is to reveal it to her whom it enables, if so she shall choose, to dislodge himself from the position which has been the great object of his desires and efforts. By simply allowing the trial and sentence of Felix to take their course, he would, to all appearance, strengthen the possibility that by p. 29marriage to Esther his position shall be maintained, with the further joy of having that "white new-winged dove" thenceforth by his side. He comes forward as witness on behalf of Felix, and gives his evidence fairly, truly, and in such guise as makes it tell most favourably for the accused, and at the same time against himself; and, last and most touching of all, it is after he knows the full depth of the humiliation in which his mother's sin has for life involved him, that his first exhibition of tenderness, sympathy, and confidence towards that poor stricken heart and blighted life comes forth. How comes it that this "well-tanned man of the world" thus always chooses the higher and more difficult right; and does this in no excitement or enthusiasm, but coolly, calculatingly, with clear forecasting of all the consequences, and fairly entitled to assume that these shall be to his own peril or detriment?

We cannot assign this seeming anomaly to that undefinable something called the instinct of the gentleman, {29} so specially recognised in the elder and younger Debarry, as a reality and power in life. To say nothing of the fact that this instinct p. 30deals primarily with questions of feeling, and only indirectly and incidentally with questions of moral right, Harold Transome, alike congenitally and circumstantially, could scarcely by possibility have been animated by it even in slight degree, nor does it ever betray its presence in him through those slight but graceful courtesies of life which are pre-eminently the sphere of its manifestation. Equally untenable is the hypothesis which ascribes these manifestations of character wholly to the influence of a nature higher than his own appealing to him — that of Felix Holt, the glorious old Dissenter, or Esther Lyon. Such appeals can have any avail only when in the nature appealed to there remains the capability to recognise that right is greater than success or joy, and the moral power of will to act on that recognition. In the fact that Harold's nature does respond to these appeals we have the clue to the apparent anomaly his character presents. We see that, howsoever overlaid by temperament and restrained by circumstance, the noblest capability in man still survives and is active in him. He *can* choose the right which imperils his own interests, because it *is* the right; he *can* set his back on the wrong which would advantage himself, because it *is* the wrong. That he does this coolly, temperately, without enthusiasm, with full, clear forecasting of all the consequences, is only saying that he is Harold Transome still. That he does so choose when the forecast probabilities are p. 31all against those objects which the mere man of the world most desires, proves that under that hard external crust dwells as essential a nobleness as any we recognise in Felix Holt. There is an inherent strength and manliness in Harold Transome to which Arthur Donnithorne or Godfrey Cass can never attain.

Few things in the literary history of the age are more puzzling than the reception given to 'Romola' by a novel-devouring public. That the lovers of mere sensationalism should not have appreciated it, was to be fully expected. But to probably the majority of readers, even of average intelligence and capability, it was, and still is, nothing but a weariness. With the more thoughtful, on the other hand, it took at once its rightful place, not merely as by far the finest and highest of all the author's works, but as perhaps the greatest and most perfect work of fiction of its class ever till then produced.

Of its artistic merits we do not propose to speak in detail. But as a historical reproduction of an epoch and a life peculiarly difficult of reproduction, we do not for a moment hesitate to say that it has no rival, except, perhaps,—and even that at a distance,—Victor Hugo's incomparably greatest work, 'Nttre Dame de Paris.' It is not that we *see* as in a panorama the Florence of the Medicis and Savonarola,—we live, we move, we feel as if actors in it. Its turbulence, its struggles for freedom and independence, its factions with their complicated transitions and changes, its p. 32conspiracies and treasons, its classical jealousies and triumphs,—we feel ourselves mixed up with them all. Names historically immortal are made to us familiar presences and voices. Its nobles and its craftsmen alike become to us as friends or foes. Its very buildings—the Duomo and the Campanile, and many another—rise in their stateliness and their grace before those who have never been privileged to see them, clear and vivid as the rude northern houses that daily obtrude on our gaze.

So distinct and all-pervading, in this great work, is what we are maintaining to be the central moral purpose of all the author's works, that it can scarcely escape the notice of the most superficial reader. Affirmatively and negatively, in Romola and Tito—the two forms of illustration to some extent combined in Savonarola—the constant, persistent, unfaltering utterance of the book is, that the only true worth and greatness of humanity lies in its pursuit of the highest truth, purity, and right, irrespective of every issue, and in exclusion of every meaner aim; and that the true debasement and hopeless loss of humanity lies in the path of self-pleasing. The form of this work, the time and country in which the scene is laid, and the selection of one of the three great actors in it, leads the author more definitely than in almost any of those which preceded it to connect her moral lesson, not merely with Christianity as a religious faith, but with that Church which, as called by the name of Christ, p. 33howsoever fallen away from its "first love," is still, in the very fact of its existence, a witness for Him. While, on the other hand, through many of its subordinate characters, we have the broad catholic truth kept ever before us, that, irrespective of all formal profession or creed, voluntary acceptance of a higher life-law than the seeking our own interests, pleasure, or will, is, according to its degree, life's best and highest fulfilment; and thus we trace Him who "pleased not Himself" as the life and the light of the world, even when that world may be least formally acknowledging Him.

The three in whom this great lesson is most prominently illustrated in the work before us are, of course, Romola herself, Tito Melema, and Savonarola. And in each the illustration is so modified, and, through the three together, so almost exhaustively accomplished, that some examination of each seems necessary to our main object in this survey of George Eliot's works.

Few, we think, can study the delineation of Romola without feeling that imagination has seldom placed before us a fairer, nobler, and completer female presence. Perfectly human and natural; unexaggerated, we might almost say unidealised, alike in her weaknesses and her nobleness; combining such deep womanly tenderness with such spotless purity; so transparent in her truthfulness; so clear in her perceptions of the true and good, so firm in her aspirations p. 34after these; so broad, gentle, and forbearing in her charity, yet so resolute against all that is mean and base;—everything fair, bright, and high in womanhood seems to combine in Romola. So true, also, is the process of her development to what is called nature—to the laws and principles that regulate human action and life—that, as it proceeds before us, we almost lose note that there is development. The fair young heathen first presented to us, linked on to classic times and moralities through all the surroundings of her life, passes on so imperceptibly into the "visible Madonna" of the after-time, that we scarcely observe the change till it is accomplished. From the first, we know that the mature is involved in the young Romola. The reason of this is, that from first to last the essential principle of life is in her the same. Equally, when she first comes before us, and in all the after-glory of her serene unconscious self-devotedness, she is living to others, not to herself.

Her first devotion is to her father. Her one passion of life is to compensate to him all he has lost: the eyes, once so full of fire, now sightless; the son and brother, who, at the call of an enthusiasm with which their nobler natures refuse to sympathise—for it was, in the first instance, but the supposed need to save his own soul—has fled from his nearest duty of life. To this devotion she consecrates her fair young existence. For this she dismisses from it all thought of ease or p. 35pleasure, and chooses retirement and isolation; gives herself to uncongenial studies and endless labours, and accepts, in uncomplaining sadness, that which to such a nature is hardest of all to bear—her father's non-appreciation of all she would be and is to him. From the first, her life is one of entire self-consecration. The sphere of its activities expands as years flow on, but the principle is throughout the same. In the exquisite simplicity, purity, and tenderness of her young love, she is Romola still. There is no self-isolation included in it. Side by side with satisfying her own yearning heart, lies the thought that she is thus giving to her father a son to replace him who has forsaken him. Her first perception of the want of perfect oneness between Tito and herself dawns upon her through no change in him towards herself, but through his less sedulous attendance on her father. And when at last the conviction is borne in upon her that between him and her, seemingly so closely united, there lies the gulf that parts truth and falsehood, heaven and hell, it is no perceptible withdrawal of his love from her that forces on her this conviction. It is his falseness and treason to the dead. Then comes the crisis of her career; her flight from the unendurable burden of that divided life; her meeting with Savonarola; and her being through him brought face to face with the Christian aspect of that deepest of all moral truths,—the precedence of duty above all else. Savonarola's demand might well p. 36seem to one such as Romola laying on her a burden too heavy to be borne. It was not that it called her to return to hardness and pain; she was going forth unshrinking into the unknown with no certainty but that these would find her there; it called her to return to what, with her high ideal of love and life, could not but seem degradation and sin,—according in the living daily lie that they two, so hopelessly parted, were one. To any lower nature the appeal would have been addressed in vain. It prevails with her because it sets before her but the extension and more perfect fulfilment of the life law toward which she has been always aiming, even through the dim light of her all but heathen nurture.

She goes back to reassume her cross: sadly, weariedly forecasting, as only such a nature can do, all its shame and pain; and even still only dimly assured that her true path lies here. The very nobleness which constrains her return makes that return the harder. The unknown into which she had thought to flee had no possibility of pain or fear for her, compared to the certain pain and difficulty of that life from which all reality of love is gone: where her earnest, truthful spirit must live in daily contact with baseness,—may even have, through virtue of her relation to Tito, tacitly to concur in treason. She goes back to what, constituted as she is, can be only a daily, lifelong crucifying, and she goes back to it knowing that such it must be.

p. 37Thenceforth goes on in her that process which, far beyond all reasonings, makes the mystery of sorrow intelligible to us,—the "making perfect through suffering." It is not necessary we should trace the process step by step. It is scarcely possible to do so, for its stages are too subtle to be so traced. We see rather by result than in operation how her path of voluntary self-consecration—of care and thought for all save self—of patient, silent, solitary endurance of her crown of thorns, is brightening more and more toward the perfect day. In the streets of the faction-torn, plague-stricken, famine-wasted city; by the side of the outraged Baldassarre; in the room of the child-mistress Tessa; most of all in that home whence all other brightness has departed,—she moves and stands more and more before us the "visible Madonna."

How sharply the sword has pierced her heart, how sorely the crown of thorns is pressing her fair young brow, we learn in part from her decisive interview with Tessa. She, the high-born lady, spotless in purity, shrinking back from the very shadow of degradation, questions the unconscious instrument of one of her many wrongs with the one anxiety and hope that she may prove to be no true wife after all; that the bond which binds her to living falsehood and baseness may be broken, though its breaking stamp her with outward dishonour and blot. Otherwise there is no obtrusion of her burning pain; no revolt of faith and trust, impeaching God of hardness and p. 38wrong toward her; no murmur in His ear, any more than in the ear of man. Meek, patient, steadfast, she devotes herself to every duty and right that life has left to her; and the dark-garmented Piagnone moves about the busy scene a white-robed ministrant of mercy and love. Ever and anon, indeed, the lonely anguish of her heart breaks forth, but in the form of expression it assumes she is emphatically herself. In those frequent touching appeals to Tito, deepening in their sweet earnestness with every failure, we may read the intensity of her ever-present inward pain. In them all the self-seeking of love has no place. The effort is always primarily directed, not toward winning back his love and confidence for herself, but toward winning him back to truth and right and loyalty of soul. Her pure high instinct knows that only so can love return between them—can the shattered bond be again taken up. She seeks to save *him*—him who will not be saved, who has already vitally placed himself out of the pale of possible salvation.

One of the most touching manifestations in this most touching of all records of feminine nobleness and suffering, is the story of her relations to Tessa. It would seem as if in that large heart jealousy, the reaching self-love of love, could find no place. Her discovery of the relation in which Tessa stands to Tito awakens first that saddest of all sad hopes in one like Romola, that through the contadina she may be p. 39released from the marriage-bond that so galls and darkens her life. When that hope is gone, no thought of Tessa as a successful rival presents itself. She thinks of her only as another victim of Tito's wrong-doing—as a weak, simple, helpless child, innocent of all conscious fault, to be shielded and cared for in the hour of need.

At last, after the foulest of Tito's treasons, which purchases safety and advancement for himself by the betrayal and death of her noble old godfather, her last living link to the past, the burden of her life becomes beyond her bearing, and again she attempts to lay it down by fleeing. There is no Savonarola now to meet and turn her back. Savonarola has lost the power, has forfeited the right, to do so. The pupil has outgrown the teacher; her self-renunciation has become simpler, purer, deeper, more entire than his. The last words exchanged between these two bring before us the change that has come over the spiritual relations between them. "The cause of my party," says Savonarola, "*is* the cause of God's kingdom." "I do not believe it," is the reply of Romola's "passionate repugnance." "God's kingdom is something wider, else let me stand without it with the beings that I love." These words tell us the secret of Savonarola's gathering weakness and of Romola's strength. Self, under the subtle form of identifying truth and right with his own party— with his own personal judgment of the cause and the course of p. 40right—has so far led *him* astray from the straight onward path. Right, in its clear, calm, direct simplicity, has become to her supreme above what is commonly called salvation itself.

It is another agency than Savonarola's now that brings her back once more to take up the full burden of her cross. She goes forth not knowing or heeding whither she goes, "drifting away" unconscious before wind and wave. These bear her into the midst of terror, suffering, and death; and there, in self-devotedness to others, in patient ministrations of love amid poverty, ignorance, and superstition, the noble spirit rights itself once more, the weary fainting heart regains its quiet steadfastness. She knows once more that no amount of wrong-doing can dissolve the bond uniting her to Tito; that no degree of pain may lawfully drive her forth from that sphere of doing and suffering which is *hers*. She returns, not in joy or hope, but in that which is deeper than all joy and hope — in love; the one thought revealed to us being that it may be her blessedness to stand by him whose baseness drove her away when suffering and loss have come upon him. But Death — the mystery to which we look as the solver of all earthly mysteries — has resolved for her this darkest and saddest perplexity of her life. Tito is gone to his place: and his baseness shall vex her no more with antagonistic duties and a divided life. There is no joy, no expressed sense of relief and release; no reproach of him other than p. 41that implied one which springs out of the necessities of her being, the putting away from her, quietly and unobtrusively, the material gains of his treasons. The poor innocent wrong-doer, Tessa, is sought for, rescued, and cared for; and is never allowed to know the foul wrong to her rescuer of which she has been made the unconscious instrument. Even to her the language is that "Naldo will return no more, not because he is cruel, but because he is dead."

One direct trial of her faith and patience remains, through the weakness and apparent apostasy of Savonarola. Has he, through whom first came to her definite guidance amid the dark perplexities of her life, been always untrue? has the light that seemed through him to dawn on her been therefore misleading and perverting? In almost agonised intentness she listens for some word, watches for some sign, which shall tell her it has not been so. She outrages all her womanly sensibilities by being present at the death-scene, in hope that something there, were it but the uplifting of the drooping head to the clear true light of heaven, shall reassure her that the prophet was a true prophet, and his voice to her the voice of God.

But she watches in vain. Without word or sign that even her quick sure instinct can interpret, Savonarola passes into "the eternal silence." What measure of overshadowing darkness and sorrow then again fell over her life we are not told: we only know how that life passed from under this cloud also into p. 42purer and serener light. This perplexity also solves itself for her in the path of unquestioning acceptance of duty, human service, and human love; and as she treads this path, the mists clear away from around Savonarola too, and she sees him again at last as he really was, in the essential truthfulness, nobleness, and self-devotedness of his life.

Of the after-life little is told us, but little needed to be told. We have followed Romola thus far with dulled intelligence of mind and soul if we cannot picture it clearly and certainly for ourselves. Love that never falters, patience that never questions, meekness that never fails, truth clear and still as the light of heaven, devotedness that knows no thought of self, a life flowing calmly on through whatever of sorrow and disappointment may remain toward the perfect purity and blessedness of heaven. Few, we think, can carefully study the character and development of Romola del Bardo and refuse to endorse the verdict that Imagination has given us no figure more rounded and complete in every grace and glory of feminine loveliness.

The sensational fiction of the day has laboured hard in the production of great criminals; but it has produced no human being so vitally debased, no nature so utterly loathsome, no soul so hopelessly lost, as the handsome, smiling, accomplished, popular, viceless Greek, Tito Melema. Yet is he the very reverse of what is called a monster of iniquity. That p. 43which gives its deep and awful power to the picture is its simple, unstrained, unvarnished truthfulness. He knows little of himself who does not recognise as existent within himself, and as always battling for supremacy there, that principle of evil which, accepted by Tito as his life-law, and therefore consummating itself in him, "bringeth forth death;" death the most utter and, so far as it is possible to see, the most hopeless that can engulf the human soul.

The conception of Tito as one great central figure in a work of art would scarcely, we think, have occurred to any one whose moral aim was other than that which it is the endeavour of these remarks to trace out in George Eliot's works. The working out of that conception, as it is here worked out, would, we believe, have been impossible to any one who had less strongly realised wherein all the true nobleness and all the true debasement of humanity lie.

Outwardly, on his first appearance, there is not merely nothing repellent about Tito; in person and manner, in genial kindly temper, in those very forms of intelligence and accomplishment that specially suit the city and the time, there is superficially everything to conciliate and attract. It is almost impossible to define the subtle threads of indication through which, from the first, we are forced to distrust him. Superficially, it might seem at this time as if with Tito the probabilities were equal as regards good and evil; and that with Romola's love thrown into the scale, p. 44their preponderance on the side of good were all but irresistible. Yet from the first we feel that it is otherwise—that this light, genial, ease-loving nature has already, by its innate habitude of self-pleasing, foreordained itself to sink down into ever deeper and more utter debasement. With the "slight, almost imperceptible start," at the accidental words which connect the value of his jewels with "a man's ransom," we feel that some baseness is already within himself contemplated. With the transference of their price to the goldsmith's hands, we know that the baseness is in his heart resolved on. When the message through the monk tells him that the ransom may still be available, we never doubt what the decision will be. Present ease and enjoyment, the maintaining and improving the position he has won—in short, the "something that is due to himself," rather than a distant, dangerous, possibly fruitless duty, howsoever clear.

The one purer feeling in that corrupt heart—his love for Romola—is almost from the first tainted by the same selfishness. From the first he recognises that his relation to her will give him a certain position in the city; and he feels that with his ready tact and Greek suppleness this is all that is needed to secure his further advancement. The vital antagonism between his nature and hers bars the possibility of his foreseeing how her truthfulness, nobleness, and purity shall become the thorn in his ease-loving life.

p. 45In his earlier relations with Tessa, there is nothing more than seeking a present and passing amusement, and the desire to sun himself in her childish admiration and delight. He is as far as possible from the intentional seducer and betrayer. But his accidental encounters with her, cause him perplexity and annoyance; and at last it seems to him safer for his own position, especially in regard to Romola, that she should be secretly housed as she is, and taught to regard herself as his wife. Soon there comes to be more of ease for him with the bond-submissive child-mistress, than in the presence of the high-souled, pure-hearted wife. In the first and decisive encounter with Baldassarre, the words of repudiation which seal the whole after-character of his life, apparently escape from him unconsciously and by surprise. But it is the traitor-heart that speaks them. They could never even by surprise have escaped the lips, had not the baseness of their denial and desertion been already in the heart consummated.

We need not follow him through all his subsequent and deepening treasons. They all, without exception, want every element that might make even treason impressive. They want even such factitious elevation as their being prompted by hatred or revenge might lend;—even such broader interest as their being done in the interest of a party, or for some wide end, could confer. They have no fuller or deeper import than the present ease, present safety, present or future advantage, p. 46of that object which fills up his universe,—Self. He would rather not have betrayed the trust reposed in him by Romola's father, if the end he thereby proposed to himself could have been attained otherwise than through such betrayal. His plot with Dolfo Spini for placing the great Monk-prophet in the hands of his enemies, has no darker motive than the getting out of the way an indirect obstacle to his own advancement, and a man whose labours tend to make life harder and more serious for all who come under his influence. Bernardo del Nero, with his stainless honour, has from the first taken up an attitude of tacit revulsion toward him; but there is no revenge prompting the part he plays towards the noble, true-hearted old man. He would rather that he and his fellow-victims were saved, if his own safety and ultimate gain could be secured otherwise than through their betrayal and death. There is no hardness or cruelty in him, save when its transient displays toward Romola are necessary for furthering some present end: he never indulges in the luxury of unnecessary and unprofitable sins. The sharp, steadfast, unwavering consistency of Tito is even more marked than that of Romola, for twice Romola falters, and turns to flee. The supple, flexible Greek follows out the law he has laid down as the law of his life,—worships the god he has set up as the god of his worship with an inexorable constancy that never for one chance moment falters. That god is self; that law is, in one word, p. 47self-pleasing. Long before the end comes, we feel that Tito Melema is a lost soul; that for him and in him there is no place for repentance; that to him we may without any uncharity apply the most fearful words human language has ever embodied;—he has sinned the "sin which *cannot* be forgiven, neither in this world, neither in the world to come."

"Justice," says the author, as the dead Tito is borne past still locked in the death-clutch of the human avenger—"justice is like the kingdom of God: it is not without us as a fact; it is within us as a great yearning." In these solemn truthful words we have suggested to us how feebly mere physical death can shadow forth that spiritual corruption, that "second death," which we have seen hour by hour consummating in him who has lived for self alone.

Few of the great figures which stand up amid the dimness of medieval history are more perplexing to historian and biographer than Savonarola. On a first glance we seem shut up to one or other of two alternatives—regarding him as an apostle and martyr, or as a charlatan. And even more careful examination leaves in his character and life anomalies so extraordinary, contradictions so inextricable, that most historians have fallen back on the hypothesis of partial insanity—the insanity born of an honest and upright but extravagant fanaticism—as the only one adequate to explain the mystery. Whether George Eliot has in this work produced a more satisfactory solution, p. 48we do not attempt formally to determine. We are sure, however, that every thoughtful reader will recognise that the solution she offers is one in strict and deep consistency with all the laws of human action, and all the tendencies of human imperfection; and that the Savonarola she places before us is a being we can understand *by sympathy*—sympathy at once with the greatness of his aims, and still more fully with the weaknesses that lead him astray.

The picture is a very impressive one, alike in its grandeur and in its sadness, speaking its true, deep, universal lesson home to us and to our life: alike when it shows us the strength and nobleness of life attuning itself to the highest good, and battling on toward the highest right; and when it shows us how self, under a form which does not seem self, may steal in to sap its strength and to abase its nobleness.

The great Monk-prophet comes upon the scene a new "voice crying in the wilderness" of selfishness and wrong around him—an impassioned witness that "there is a God that judgeth in the earth," protesting by speech and by life against the self-seeking and self-pleasing he sees on every side. To the putting down of this, to the living his own life, to the rousing all men to live theirs, not to pleasure, but to God; merging all private interests in the public good, and that the best good; looking each one not to his own pleasures, ambition, or ease, but to that which shall best advance a reign of truth, justice, and love on p. 49earth,—to this end he has consecrated himself and all his powers. The path thus chosen is for himself a hard one; circumstanced as our humanity is, it never has been otherwise—never shall be so while these heavens and this earth remain. Mere personal self-denials, mere turning away from the outward pomps and vanities of the world, lie very lightly on a nature like Savonarola's, and such things scarcely enter into the pain and hardness of his chosen lot. It is the opposition,—active, in the intrigues and machinations of enemies both in Church and State—passive, in the dull cold hearts that respond so feebly and fitfully to his appeals; it is the constant wearing bitterness of hope deferred, the frequent still sterner bitterness of direct disappointment,—it is things like these that make his cross so heavy to bear. But they cannot turn him aside from his course—cannot win him to lower his aim to something short of the highest good conceivable by him. We may smile now in our days of so-called enlightenment at some of the measures he directs in pursuance of his great aim. His "Pyramid of Vanities" may be to our self-satisfied complacency itself a vanity. To him it represents a stern reality of reformation in character and life; and to the Florentine of his age it symbolises one form of vain self-pleasing offered up in solemn willing sacrifice to God.

One trial of his faith and steadfastness, long expected, comes on him at last. The recognised head p. 50of that great organisation of which he is a vowed and consecrated member declares against him, and the papal sentence of excommunication goes forth. We, looking as we deem on the Papacy trembling to its fall, can very imperfectly enter into the awful gravity of this struggle. To us, the prohibition of an Alexander Borgia may seem of small account, and his anathema of small weight in the councils of the universe. But it was otherwise with Savonarola: the Monk-apostle, trained and vowed to unqualified obedience, has thus forced on him the most difficult problem of his time. This to him more than earthly authority, the visible embodiment of the Divine on earth, the direct and only representative of the one authority of God in Christ, has declared his course to be a course of error and sin. Shall he accept or reject the decision? To reject, is to break with the supposed tradition of fourteen centuries, and with all his own past training, predilections, and habits of thought; it is to nullify his own voluntary act of the past, accepting implicit obedience, and to go forth on a path which has thenceforth no outward guidance, light, or stay. To accept, is to break with all his own truest and deepest past, to abandon all that for him gives truth and reality to life, and to retire to his cell, and limit his attention thenceforth—if he can—to making the "salvation" of his own soul secure. We may safely esteem that this is the culminating struggle of his life. We may well understand the solemn pause p. 51that ensues, the retirement to solitude, there to review the position before the only court of appeal that remains to him,—that inward voice of conscience, that inward sense of right, which is the immediate presence of God within. But we never doubt what the decision will be. "I must obey God rather than man; I cannot recognise that this voice—even of God's vicegerent—is the voice of God. Necessity is laid on me, which I dare not gainsay, to preach this Gospel of God's kingdom, as, even on earth, a kingdom of righteousness, truth, and love."

Such is one phase of the Savonarola here portrayed to us; and herein is placed before us the secret of his greatness and strength. This firm assertion of the highest right his consciousness recognises, amid all difficulty, hardness, and disappointment; this persistent endeavour by precept and example to rouse men to a truer and better life than their own varied self-seekings; this unflinching struggle against everything false, mean, and base,—these things make him a power in the State before which King and Pope are compelled to bow in respect or fear. Over even the larger nature of Romola his words at this time have sway,—the sway which more distinct perception of *all* the relations of duty gives over a spirit equally earnest to seek the right alone.

In time there comes a change, almost imperceptibly, working from within outwards, first clearly announced through the changed relations of others to him, though p. 52these are but symptomatic of change within himself. The political strength of his sway is broken, its moral strength is all but gone. The nature of the change in himself he unwittingly defines in those last words to Romola already quoted, "The cause of *my party* is the cause of God's kingdom." Various external circumstances have contributed to bring about the result thus indicated; but on these it is unnecessary to dwell. God's kingdom has lowered and narrowed itself into his party. The spirit of the partisan has begun to overshadow the purity of the patriot, to contract and abase the wide aim of the Christian; and he has come to substitute a law of right modified to suit the interests of the party, for that law which is absolute and unconditional. He whom we listened to in the Duomo as the fervid proclaimer of God's justice, stands now before us as the perverter of even human justice and human law. The very nobleness of Bernardo del Nero strengthens the necessity that he should die, that the Mediceans may be thus deprived of the support of his stainless honour and high repute; though to compass this death the law of mercy which Savonarola himself has instituted must be put aside. As we listen to the miserable sophistries by which he strives to justify himself—far less to Romola than before his own accusing soul—we feel that the greatness of his strength has departed from him. All thenceforth is deepening confusion without and within. Less and less can he control the violences of his party, p. 53till these provoke all but universal revolt, and the "Masque of the Furies" ends his public career. The uncertainties and vacillations of the "Trial by Fire," the long series of confessions and retractations, historically true, are still more morally and spiritually significant. They tell of inward confusion and perplexity, generated through that partial "self-pleasing" which, under guise so insidious, had stolen into the inner life; of faith and trust perturbed and obscured thereby; of dark doubts engendered whether God had indeed ever spoken by him. We feel it is meet the great life should close, not as that of the triumphant martyr, but amid the depths of that self-renouncing penitence through which once more the soul resumes its full relation to the divine.

* * * * *

We have now come to the one great poem George Eliot has as yet given to the world, and which we have no hesitation in placing above every poetical or poetico-dramatic work of the day—'The Spanish Gypsy.' Less upon it than upon any of its predecessors can we attempt any general criticism. Our attention must be confined mainly to two of the great central figures of the drama—Fedalma herself, and Don Silva; the representatives respectively of humanity accepting the highest, noblest, most self-devoting life presented to it, simultaneously with life's deepest pain; and of humanity choosing something—p. 54in itself pure and noble, but—short of the highest.

Fedalma is essentially a poetic Romola, but Romola so modified by circumstances and temperament as to be superficially contrasting. She is the Romola of a different race and clime, a different nurture, and an era which, chronologically nearly the same, is in reality far removed. For the warm and swift Italian we have the yet warmer and swifter Gypsy blood; for the long line of noble ancestry, descent from an outcast and degraded race; for the nurture amid the environments, almost in the creed of classicism, the upbringing under noble female charge in a household of that land where the Roman Church had just sealed its full supremacy by the establishment of the Inquisition; for the era when Italian subtleties of thought, policy, and action had attained their highest elaboration, the grander and simpler time when

> "Castilian gentlemen
> *Choose* not their task—they choose *to do it well*."

But howsoever modified through these and other accessories of existence are the more superficial aspects of character, and the whole outward form and course of life, the great vital principle is the same in both;—clearness to see, nobleness to choose, steadfastness to pursue, the highest good that life presents, through whatsoever anguish, darkness, and death of all joy and hope the path may lead.

p. 55On Fedalma's first appearance on the wonderful scene upon the Plaga, she presents herself as emphatically what her poet-worshipper Juan hymns her, the "child of light"—a creature so tremulously sensitive to all beauty, brightness, and joy, that it seems as if she could not co-exist with darkness and sorrow. But even then we have intimated to us that vital quality in her nature which makes all self-sacrifice possible; and which assures us that, whenever her life-choice shall come to lie between enjoyment and right, she shall choose the higher though the harder path. For her joy is essentially the joy of sympathy; mere self has no place in it. In her exquisite justification of the Plaga scene to Don Silva, she herself defines it in one line better than all words of ours can do—

"*I* was not, but joy was, and love and triumph."

She is but a form and presence in which the joy, not merely of the fair sunset scene, but primarily and emphatically of the human hearts around her, enshrines itself. It has no free life in herself apart from others; it must inevitably die if shut out from this tremulousness of human sympathy. And we know it shall give place to a sorrow correspondingly sensitive, intense, and absorbing, whenever the young bright spirit is brought face to face with human sorrow. Even while we gaze on her as the embodied joy, and love, and triumph of the scene, the shadow begins to fall. The band of Gypsy prisoners passes by, and her eyes meet p. 56those eyes whose gaze, not to be so read by any nature lower and more superficial than hers—

"Seemed to say he bore
The pain of those who never could be saved."

Joy collapses at once within her; the light fades away from the scene; the very sunset glory becomes dull and cold. We are shown from the first that no life can satisfy this "child of light" which shall not be a life in the fullest and deepest unison to which circumstances shall call her with the life of humanity. That true greatness of our humanity is already active within her, which makes it impossible she should live or die to herself alone. Her destiny is already marked out by a force of which circumstance may determine the special manifestation, but which no force of circumstance can turn aside from its course; the force of a living spiritual power within herself which constrains that she shall be faithful to the highest good which life shall place before her.

We would fain linger for a little over the scenes which follow between her and Don Silva; portraying as they do a love so intense in its virgin tenderness, and so spiritually pure and high. It is the same "child of light" that comes before us here; the same tremulous living in the light and joy of her love, but also the same impossibility of living even in its light and joy apart from those of her beloved. And not from his only: that passion which in more p. 57ordinary natures so almost inevitably contracts the sphere of the sympathies, in Fedalma expands and enlarges it. Amid all the intoxicating sweetness of her bright young joys, the loving heart turns again and again to the thought of human sorrow and wrong; and among all the hopes that gladden her future, one is never absent from her thoughts— "Oh! I shall have much power as well as joy;" power to redress the wrong and to assuage the suffering. Half playfully, half seriously, she asks the question—

> "But is it *what* we love, or *how* we love,
> That makes true good?"

Most seriously and solemnly is the question answered through her after-life. To love less wholly, purely, unselfishly—yet still holding the outward claims of that love subordinate to a possible still higher and more imperative claim—to such a nature as hers is no love and no true good at all. And this thirst for the highest alike in love and life includes her lover as well as herself. The darkest terror that overtakes her in all those after-scenes comes when he is about to abjure country, honour, and God on her account. To her, the Gypsy, without a country, without a faith save faithfulness to the highest right, without a God such as the Spaniards' God, this might be a small thing. But for him, Spanish noble and Christian knight, she knows it to be abnegation of nobleness, treason to duty, dishonour and shame. She is jealous p. 58for his truth, but the more that its breach might seem to secure her own happiness.

The first and decisive scene with her Gypsy father is so true in conception, and so full of poetic force and grandeur throughout, that no analysis, nothing short of extracting the whole, can do justice to it. Seldom before has art in any guise placed the grand, heroic, self-devoting purpose of a grand, heroic, self-devoting nature more impressively before us than in the Gypsy chief. It is easy to think and speak of such an enterprise as Quixotic and impossible. There is a stage in every great enterprise humanity has ever undertaken when it might be so characterised: and the greatest of all enterprises, when an obscure Jew stood forth to become light and life, not to a tribe or a race, but to humanity, was to the judgers according to appearance of His day, the most Quixotic and impossible of all.

It has been felt and urged as an objection to this scene, and consequently to the whole scheme of the drama, that such influence, so immediately exerted over Fedalma by a father whom till then she had never known, is unnatural if not impossible. If it were only as father and daughter they thus stand face to face, there might be force in the objection. But this very partially and inadequately expresses the relation between these two. It is the father possessed with a lofty, self-devoting purpose, who calls to share in, and to aid it, the daughter whose nature is strung p. 59to the same lofty, self-devoting pitch. It is the saviour of an oppressed, degraded, outcast race, who calls to share his mission her who could feel the brightness of her joy of love brightened still more by the hope of assuaging sorrow and redressing evil. It is the appeal through the father of that which is highest and noblest in humanity to that which is most deeply inwrought into the daughter's soul. To a narrower and meaner nature the appeal would have been addressed by any father in vain: for a narrower and meaner end, the appeal even by such a father would have been addressed to Fedalma in vain. With her it cannot but prevail, unless she is content to forego—not merely her father's love and trust, but—her own deepest and truest life.

The "child of light," the embodied "joy and love and triumph" of the Plaga, is called on to forego all outward and possible hope on behalf of that love which is for her the concentration of all light and joy and triumph. Very touching are those heart-wrung pleadings by which she strives to avert the sacrifice; and we are oppressed almost as by the presence of the calm, loveless, hateless Fate of the old Greek tragedy, as Zarca's inexorable logic puts them one by one aside, and leaves her as sole alternatives the offering up every hope, every present and possible joy of the love which is entwined with her life, or the turning away from that highest course to which he calls her. As her own young hopes die out under the pressure of p. 60that deepest energy of her nature to which he appeals, it can hardly be but that all hope should grow dull and cold within—hope even with regard to the issue of that mission to which she is called; and it is thus that she accepts the call:—

> "Yes, say that we shall fail. I will not count
> On aught but being faithful. . . .
> I will seek nothing but to shun base joy.
> The saints were cowards who stood by to see
> Christ crucified. They should have thrown them-
> selves
> Upon the Roman spears, and died in vain.
> The grandest death, to die in vain, for love
> Greater than rules the courses of the world.
> Such death shall be my bridegroom. . . .
> Oh love! you were my crown. No other crown
> Is aught but thorns on this poor woman's brow."

In this spirit she goes forth to meet her doom, faithfulness thenceforth the one aim and struggle of her life—faithfulness to be maintained under the pressure of such anguish of blighted love and stricken hope as only natures so pure, tender, and deep can know—faithfulness clung to with but the calmer steadfastness when the last glimmer of mere hope is gone.

The successive scenes in the Gypsy camp with Juan, with her father, and with the Gypsy girl Hinda, bring before us at once the intensity of her suffering and the depth of her steadfastness. Trembling beneath the burden laid upon her,—laid on her by p. 61no will of another, but by the earnestness of her own humanity,—we see her seeking through Juan whatever of possible comfort can come through tidings of him she has left; in the strong and noble nature of her father, the consolation of at least hoping that her sacrifice shall not be all in vain; and in Hinda's untutored, instinctive faithfulness to her name and race, support to her own resolve. But no pressure of her suffering, no despondency as to the result of all, no thought of the lonely life before her, filled evermore with those yearnings toward the past and the vanished, can turn her back from her chosen path.

> "Father, my soul is weak,
>
> . . . .
> But if I cannot plant resolve on hope,
> It will stand firm on certainty of woe.
> . . . Hopes have precarious life;
> But faithfulness can feed on suffering,
> And knows no disappointment. Trust in me.
> If it were needed, this poor trembling hand
> Should grasp the torch—strive not to let it fall,
> Though it were burning down close to my flesh.
> No beacon lighted yet. I still should hear
> Through the damp dark the cry of gasping swim-
> mers.
> Father, I will be true."

The scenes which follow, first with her lover, then with her lover and her father together, present the culmination at once of her trial and of her steadfastness. Hitherto she has made her choice, as it were, in the bodily absence of that love, the abnegation of p. 62whose every hope gives its sharpness to her crown of thorns. Now the light and the darkness, the joy and the sorrow, the love whose earthly life she is slaying, and the life of lonely, ceaseless, lingering pain before her, stand, as it were, visibly and tangibly side by side. On the one hand her father, with his noble presence, his calm unquestioning self-devotion, his fervid eloquence, and his withering scorn of everything false and base, represents that deepest in humanity—and in her—which impels to seek and to cling to the highest good. On the other her lover, associated with all the deeply-cherished life, joy, and hope of her past, pleads with his earnest, impassioned, almost despairing eloquence, for her return to *happiness*. More nobly beautiful by far in her sad steadfastness than when she glowed before us as the "child of light" upon the Plaga, —

> "Her choice was made.
>
> . . . .
> Slowly she moved to choose sublimer pain,
> Yearning, yet shrinking: . . .
> . . . firm to slay her joy,
> That cut her heart with smiles beneath the knife,
> Like a sweet babe foredoomed by prophecy."

To all the despairing pleadings and appeals of her lover she has but one answer: —

> "You must forgive Fedalma all her debt.
> She is quite beggared. If she gave herself,
> 'Twould be a self corrupt with stifled thoughts
> p. 63Of a forsaken better. . . .
> Oh, all my bliss was in our love, but now
> I may not taste it; some deep energy
> Compels me to choose hunger."

What that energy is, we surely do not need to ask. It is that deep principle of all true life which represents the affinity — latent, oppressed by circumstances, repressed by sin, but always there — between our human nature and the Divine, and through subjection to which we reassume our birthright as "the sons of God"; conscience to see and will to choose — not what shall please ourselves, but — the highest and purest aim that life presents to us.

It is the same "deep energy," the same inexorable necessity of her nature, that she should put away from her all beneath the best and purest, which originates the sudden terror that smiles upon her when Don Silva, for her sake, breaks loose from country and faith, from honour and God. There is no triumph in the greatness of the love thus displayed; no rejoicing in prospect of the outward fulfilment of the love thus made possible; no room for any emotion but the dark chill foreboding of a separation thus begun, wider than all distance, and more profound and hopeless than death. The separation of aims no longer single, of souls no longer one; of his life falling, though for her sake, from its best and highest, and therefore ceasing, inevitably and hopelessly, fully to respond to hers.

> p. 64"What the Zmncala may not quit for you,
> I cannot joy that you should quit for her."

The last temptation has now been met and conquered. Henceforth we see Fedalma only in her calm, sad, unwavering steadfastness, bearing, without moan or outward sign, the burden of her cross. Not even her father's dying charge is needed to confirm her purpose, to fix her life in a self-devotedness already fixed beyond all relaxing and all change. With his death, indeed, the last faint hope fades utterly away that his great purpose shall be achieved; and she thenceforth is

> "But as the funeral urn that bears
> The ashes of a leader."

But necessity lies only the more upon her — that most imperious of all necessities which originates in her own innate nobleness — that she should be *true*. When first she accepted this burden of her nobleness and her sorrow, she had said —

> "I will not count
> On aught but being faithful;"

and faithfulness without hope — truthfulness without prospect, almost without possibility, of tangible fulfilment — is all that lies before her now. She accepts it in a mournful stillness, not of despair, and not of resignation, but simply as the only true accomplishment of her life that now remains.

p. 65The last interview with Don Silva almost oppresses us with its deep severe solemnity. No bitterness of separation broods over it: the true bitterness of separation fell upon her when her lover became false to himself in the vain imagination that, so doing, he could by any possibility be fully true to her. "Our marriage rite" — thus she addresses the repentant and returning renegade —

> "Our marriage rite
> Is our resolve that we will each be true
> To high allegiance, higher than our love;"

and it is thus she answers for herself, and teaches him to answer, that question asked in the fullest and fairest flush of her love's joys and hopes—

> "But is it what we love, or how we love,
> That makes true good?"

The tremulous sensitiveness of her former life has now passed beyond all outward manifestation, lost in absorbing self-devotedness and absorbing sorrow; and every thought, feeling, and word is characterised by an ineffable depth of calm.

Those closing lines, whose still, deep, melancholy cadence lingers upon ear and heart as do the concluding lines of 'Paradise Lost'—

> "Straining he gazed, and knew not if he gazed
> On aught but blackness overhung with stars"—

tell us how Fedalma passes away from the sight, the p. 66life, and all but the heart of Don Silva. Not thus does she pass away from our gaze. One star overhanging the blackness, clear and calm beyond all material brightness of earth and firmament, for us marks out her course: the star of unwavering faith, unfaltering truth, self-devotion to the highest and holiest that knows no change for ever.

> "A man of high-wrought strain, fastidious
> In his acceptance, dreading all delight
> That speedy dies and turns to carrion.
> . . . . . .
> A nature half-transformed, with qualities
> That oft bewrayed each other, elements
> Not blent but struggling, breeding strange effects.
> . . . . . A spirit framed
> Too proudly special for obedience,
> Too subtly pondering for mastery:
> Born of a goddess with a mortal sire;
> Heir of flesh-fettered weak divinity.
> . . . A nature quiveringly poised
> In reach of storms, whose qualities may turn
> To murdered virtues that still walk as ghosts
> Within the shuddering soul and shriek remorse."

Such is Duke Silva: and in this portraiture is up-folded the dark and awful story of his life. Noble, generous, chivalrous; strong alike by mind and by heart to cast off the hard and cruel superstition of his age and country; capable of a love pure, deep, trustful, and to all appearance self-forgetting, beyond what men are usually capable of; trenching in every p. 67quality close on the true heroic: he yet falls as absolutely short of it as a man can do who has not, like Tito Melema, by his own will coalescing with the unchangeable laws of right, foreordained himself to utter and hopeless spiritual death. It was, perhaps, needful he should be portrayed as thus nearly approaching true nobility; otherwise such perfect love from such a nature as Fedalma's were inexplicable, almost impossible. But this was still more needful toward the fulfilment of the author's purpose: the showing how the one deadly plague-spot shall weaken the strongest and vitiate the purest life. Every element of the heroic is there except that one element without which the truly heroic is impossible: he cannot "deny himself." Superficially, indeed, it might seem that self was not the object of his regard, but Fedalma: and by much of the distorted, distorting, and radically immoral fiction of the day, his sacrifice of everything for her love's sake would have been held up to us as the crowning glory of his heroism, and the consummation of his claims upon our sympathy and admiration. George Eliot has seen with a different and a clearer eye: and in Duke Silva's placing—not his love, but—the earthly fulfilment of his love above honour and faith, she finds at the root the same vital corruption of self-pleasing which conducts Tito Melema through baseness on baseness, and treason after treason, to the lowest deep of perdition.

Throughout the first wonderful love-scene with p. 68Fedalma, the vital difference, the essential antagonism between these two natures, is revealed to us through a hundred subtle and delicate touches, and we are made to feel that there is a depth in hers beyond the power of his to reach. Chivalrous, absorbing, tyrannising over his whole being, even pure as his love is, it far fails of the deeper and holier purity of hers. It shudders at the possibility of even outward soil upon her loveliness; but it does so primarily because such soil would react upon his self-love:—

> "Have *I* not made your place and dignity
> The very height of my ambition?"

Her nobler nature recoils with chill foreboding terror from his first breach of trust, *because* it is a fall from his truest and highest right. His answer to her question already quoted, reveals a love which the world's judgment may rank as the best and noblest, but reveals a principle which, applied to aught beneath the only and supremest good, makes love only a more insidious and deeply corrupting form of self-pleasing: "'Tis what I love determines how I love." Love is his "highest allegiance"; and it becomes ere long an allegiance before which truth, faith, and honour give way, and guidance and control of conscience are swept before the fierce storm of self-willed passion that brooks no interposition between itself and its aim.

We are not attempting a formal review of this work; p. 69and as we have passed without notice the powerful embodiment in Father Isidor of whatever was true and earnest in the Inquisition, we must also pass very slightly over the interview with a still more remarkable creation—the Hebrew physician and astrologer Sephardo—except as we have in this interview further illustration of the character of Don Silva, and of the direction in which the self-love of passion is impelling him. We see conscience seeking from Sephardo—and seeking in vain—confirmation of the purpose already determined in his own heart; striving toward self-justification by every sophistry the passion-blinded intellect can suggest; struggling to transfer to another the wrong, if not the shame, of his own contemplated breach of trust; endeavouring to take refuge in stellar and fatalistic agencies from his own "nature quiveringly poised" between good and evil; and at last, merging all sophistries and all influences in the fierce resolve of the self-love which has made Fedalma the one aim, glory, and crown of his life. Throughout all the apparent struggle and uncertainty, we never doubt how all shall end. Amid all the appearances of vacillation, all the seeking external aid and furtherance, we see that the resolve is fixed, that the eager passionate self which identifies Fedalma as its inalienable right and property will prevail—prevail even to set aside every obstacle of duty and right which shall seem to interpose between it and realisation.

p. 70Equally and profoundly characteristic is the position he mentally takes up with regard to the Gypsy chief, as well as Fedalma herself. Not simply or primarily from mere arrogance of rank does he assume it as a certainty that he has but to find Fedalma to win her back to his side; that he has but to lay before Zarca the offer of his rank, wealth, and influence on behalf of the outcast race, to win him to forego his purpose and to surrender the daughter whom he has called to the same lofty aim. It is because of the impossibility, swayed and tossed by the self-will of passion as he is, of his rising to the height of their nobleness; the impossibility of his realising natures so possessed by a great, heroic, self-devoting thought, that hope, joy, happiness become of little or no account in the scale, and even what is called success dwindles into insignificance, or fades away altogether from regard.

The first betrayal of his trust, the first fall from truth and honour, has been accomplished. Conscience has begun to succumb to self—self under the guise of Fedalma and the overmastering self-will which refuses to resign his claim upon her. He has secretly deserted his post, transferring to another's hands the trust which was his, and only his. A slight offence it may appear—a mere error of judgment swayed by devoted love—to leave for a day or two when no danger seems specially impending, and to leave in the hands of the trusted and loving friend the charge committed to him. A slight offence, but p. 71it has been done in direct violation of conscience, and so in practical abnegation of God. Therefore the flood-gate is opened, and all sweeps swiftly, resistlessly, remedilessly on towards catastrophe.

The tender beauty of the brief scene with Fedalma is for her overcast, and hope, the highest hope, dies out within her, when she knows that her lover, in apparent faithfulness to her, has been false to himself. From that hour for her,

> "Our joy is dead, and only smiles on us,
> A loving shade from out the place of tombs."

Then comes the interposition of the Gypsy chief, Fedalma's sweet sad steadfastness to her "high allegiance, higher than our love;" the brief moment of suspense, when

> "His will was prisoner to the double grasp
> Of rage and hesitancy;" —

and then before the stormful revulsion of baffled and despairing passion all else is swept away, and there only survives in the self-clouded mind and soul the fixed resolve to secure that which for him has come to overmaster all allegiance. Strange and sad beyond all description are the sophistries under which the sinner strives to veil his sin, — by which to silence that still small voice which will not be hushed amid all that inward moil. Fedalma's earnest pleadings with his better self, Zarca's calm, pitying, almost sorrowful scorn —

> p. 72 "*Our* poor faith
> Allows not rightful choice save of the right
> Our birth has made for us" —

fall unheeded amid that fierce tempest of aroused self-will; and the Spanish knight and noble of that very age when

> "Castilian gentlemen
> Choose not their task — they choose to do it well,"

becomes the renegade, abjuring and forswearing country, honour, and God.

We have hitherto abstained from quotation, except where necessary to illustrate our remarks. But we cannot forbear extracting from this scene the most exquisite of the many beautiful lyrics scattered throughout the poem, expressing, as it does, with a mystic power and depth beyond what the most elaborate commentary could do, the all but hopelessness of return from such a fall as Don Silva's: —

> "Push off the boat,
> Quit, quit the shore,
> The stars will guide us back: —
> O gathering cloud,
> O wide, wide sea,
> O waves that keep no track!
>
> On through the pines!
> The pillared woods,
> Where silence breathes sweet breath: —
> O labyrinth,

O sunless gloom,
The other side of death!"

p. 73In the scenes which follow among the Gypsy guard, both that with Juan and the lonely night immediately preceding the march, the terrible reaction has already begun to set in. The "quivering" poise of Don Silva's nature makes it impossible he should rest quiet in this utterness of moral and spiritual fall. Already we hear and see the "murdered virtues" begin

"To walk as ghosts
Within the shuddering soul and shriek remorse."

The past returns on him with tyrannous power,—early associations, the taking up of his knightly vows with all its grand religious and heroic accompaniments, the delegated and accepted trust which he has by forsaking betrayed—

"The life that made
His full-formed self, as the impregnant sap
Of years successive frames the full-branched
tree" —

all come back with stern reproach and denunciation of the apostate who, in hope of the outward realisation of a human love, has cast off and forsworn them all. Fiercely he fronts and strives to silence the accusing throng. Still the same plea—

"My sin was made for me
By men's perverseness:"

still the same impulses of mad, despairing self-assertion—

p. 74"I have a *right* to choose my good or ill,
A right to damn myself!" —

still the same vain imagination that union is any longer possible between Fedalma's high self-abnegating truth and his self-seeking abnegation of all truth, coupled with the arrogant assumption that he, morally so weak and fallen, can sustain her steadfast and heroic strength—"I with my love will be her providence."

When with the fearful Gypsy chant and curse

"The newer oath
Thrusts its loud presence on him,"

we feel that any madness of act the wild conflict within may dictate has become possible; and we follow to that presence of Fedalma which is now the only goal life has left to him, prepared for such outbreak of despair as shall be commensurate with a life called to such nobleness of deed and fallen to such a depth of ruin. We see the trust he has deserted in the hands of the foe against whom he had accepted commission to guard it; his friends slaughtered at the post he had forsaken; himself as the sworn Zmncalo in alliance with the enemy and slaughterer, and associated with the havoc they have wrought. The "right to damn" himself which he had claimed is his in all its bitterness; and when he would charge the self damnation upon the Gypsy chief, the reply of p. 75calm withering scorn can but add keener pang to his awaking remorse: the self-damning

"Deed was done
Before you took your oath, or reached our camp,
Done when you slipped in secret from the post
'Twas yours to keep, and not to meditate
If others might not fill it."

The climax of his revulsion, remorse, and despair is reached when the Prior, the man whom he has impeached as the true author of all his sin, is led forth to die. Then all sophistries are swept away, and the full import of his deed glares up before him, and its import as *his*, only and wholly his. Zarca, in his high self-possession of soul, almost pitying while he cannot but despise, presents a fitting object on which all the fierce conflicting passions of wrath, self-accusing remorse, and despair, may vent themselves; and the sudden and treacherous deed, which

"Strangles one
Whom ages watch for vainly,"

gives also to Don Silva himself to carry

"For ever with him what he fled —
Her murdered love — her love, a dear wronged ghost,
Facing him, beauteous, 'mid the throngs of hell."

Few authors or artists but George Eliot could have won us again to look on Don Silva except with revulsion or disgust; and it is characteristic of more p. 76than all ordinary power that through the deep impressive solemnity of the closing scene, he, the renegade and murderer, almost divides our interest and sympathy with Fedalma herself; and this by no condoning of his guilt, no extenuation of the depth of his fall, for these are here, most of all, kept ever before our eyes. But the better and nobler elements of his nature, throughout all his degradation revealed to us as never wholly overborne, as ever struggling to assert themselves, have begun to prevail, and to put down from supremacy that meaner self which has led him into such abysses of faithlessness, apostasy, and sin. The wild despair of remorse is giving way to the self-renunciation of repentance; the storm of conflicting passions and emotions is stilled; the fearful battle between good and evil through which he has passed has left him exhausted of every hope and aim save to die, repentant and absolved, for the country and faith he had abjured. The self-assertion, too, of love is gone, and only its deep purity and tenderness remain. Without murmur or remonstrance, he acquiesces in the doom of hopeless separation; accepting all that remains possible to him of that "high allegiance higher than our love," which is thenceforth the only bond of union between these two. In that last sad interview with her for whom he had so fearfully sinned, and so all but utterly fallen, we can regard Don Silva with a fuller and truer sympathy than we dare accord to him in all the height of his greatness, and p. 77all the wealth, beauty, and joy of his yet unshadowed love.

* * * * *

In the next of this series of great works, and the one which to many of her readers is and will remain the most fascinating — 'Middlemarch' — George Eliot has stretched a broader and more crowded canvas, on which, however, every figure, to the least important that appears, is — not sketched or outlined, but — filled in with an intense and lifelike vividness and precision that makes each stand out as if it stood there alone. Quote but a few words from any one of the speakers, and we know in a moment who that speaker is. And each is the type or representative of a class; we have no monsters or unnatural creations among them. To a certain extent all are idealised for good or for evil,—it cannot be otherwise in fiction without its ceasing to be fiction; but the essential elements of character and life in all are not peculiar to them, but broad and universal as our humanity itself. Dorothea and her sister, Mr Brooke and Sir James Chettam, Rosamond Vincy and her brother, Mr Vincy and his wife, Casaubon and Lydgate, Farebrother and Ladislaw, Mary Garth and her parents, Bulstrode and Raffles, even Drs Sprague and Minchin, old Featherstone and his kindred—all are but representative men and women, with whose prototypes every reader, if gifted with the subtle power of penetration and analysis of George Eliot, might claim personal acquaintance.

p. 78This richly-crowded canvas presents to us such variety of illustration of the two great antagonistic principles of human life—self-pleasing and self-abnegation, love of pleasure and the love of God more or less absolute and consummate—that it is no easy task to select from among them. But two figures stand out before us, each portrayed with such finished yet unlaboured art—living, moving, talking before us—contrasted with such exquisite yet unobtrusive delicacy, and so subtilely illustrating the two great phases of human inspiration and life—that which centres in self, and that which yearns and seeks to lose itself in the infinite of truth, purity, and love—that instinctively and irresistibly the mind fixes upon them. These are Dorothea and Rosamond Vincy.

To not a few of George Eliot's readers, we believe that Dorothea is and will always be a fairer and more attractive form than Dinah Morris or Romola di Bardi, Fedalma or Mirah Cohen. In her sweet young enthusiasm, often unguided or misguided by its very intensity, but always struggling and tending on toward the highest good; in the touching maidenly simplicity with which she at once identifies and accepts Mr Casaubon as her guide and support toward a higher, less self-contained and self-pleasing, more inclusive and all-embracing life; in the yearning pain with which the first dread of possible disappointment dawns and darkens over her, and the meek humility of her repentance on the one faint betrayal—wrung from her p. 79by momentary anguish—of that disappointment; in the tender wifely patience, reticence, forbearance, with which she hides from all, the heart-gnawings of shattered and expiring hope; the sense which she can no longer veil from her own deepest consciousness that in Mr Casaubon there is no help or stay for her and the unwearied though too soon unhoping earnestness with which she labours to establish true relations between herself and her uncongenial mate; in the patient yet crushing anguish of that long night's heart-struggle which precedes the close—a struggle not against her own higher self, but whether she dare bind down that higher self to a lifelong, narrow, worthless task, and the aching consciousness of what—almost against conscience and right—her answer must be;—there is an inexpressible charm and loveliness in all this which no one, not utterly dead to all that is fairest and best in womanhood, can fail to recognise.

Not less wonderfully depicted is the guileless frankness which, from first to last, characterises her whole relations to Ladislaw. If there is one flaw in this noble work, it is that Ladislaw on first examination is scarcely equal to this exquisite creation. Yet it might have been nearly as difficult even for George Eliot to satisfy our instinctive cravings in this particular with regard to Dorothea, as in respect to Romola or Fedalma. And when we study her portrait of Ladislaw more carefully, there is a latent p. 80beauty and nobleness about him; an innate and intense reverence for the highest and purest, and an unvarying aim and struggle toward it; an utter scorn and loathing of everything mean and base,—that almost makes us cancel the word flaw. We recognise this nobleness of nature almost on his first appearance, in the deep reverence with which he regards Dorothea, the fulness with which he penetrates the guileless candour of the relation she assumes to him, the entireness of his trust in the spotless purity of her whole nature. And in him we have presented all those essential and fundamental elements of nature which give assurance that, Dorothea by his side, he shall be no unfitting helpmeet to her, no drag or hindrance on her higher life; that he shall rise to the elevation and purity of her self-consecration, and shall stand by her side sustaining, guiding, expanding that life of ever-growing fulness and human helpfulness to which each is dedicated.

But the essence of all this moral and spiritual loveliness is its unconsciousness. Self has no place in it. From the first the one absorbing life aim and action is toward others—toward aiding the toils, advancing the well-being, relieving the suffering, elevating the life,

of all around her. And this in no spirit of self-satisfied and vainglo-
rious self-estimation, but in that utter unconsciousness which is
characteristic of her whole being. Of the social reformer, the pur-
posed philanthropist, the benefactor of the poor, the p. 81wretched,
and the fallen, there is no trace in Dorothea Brooke. Grant that, as
she is first presented to us, that aim is for the time apparently concentrated in improved cottage accommodation for the poor; even
here there is no thought of displaying the skill of the design and
contriver: there is thought alone of the object she seeks—
ameliorating the condition of those she yearns to benefit.

In her very first interview with Casaubon, there is something in-
expressibly touching in the humility of childlike trust with which
she accepts him and his "great mind," and the innocent purity with
which she allows herself to indulge the vision of a life passed by his
side; a life which he, by his influence and guidance, is to make more
full and free, and delivered from those conventionalities of custom
and fashion which restrict it. At last his cold, formal proposal of
marriage is made. She sees nothing of its true character—that he is
but seeking, not an helpmeet for life and soul in all their higher
requirements, but simply and solely a kind of superior, blindly
submissive dependant and drudge. In the *impossibility* of marriage
presenting itself to her purity of maiden innocence as a mere establishment in life, or in any of those meaner aspects in which meaner
natures regard it, she sees nothing of all this—nothing save that the
yearning of her heart is fulfilled, and that henceforth her life shall
pass under a higher guardianship, sustained by a holier strength,
animated by a p. 82more self-expansive fulness, guided toward
nobler and fuller aims.

Picturing to some extent, in degree as we are capable of entering
into a nature like hers, the anguish that such an awakening must be
to her, it is exquisitely painful to follow in imagination the slow
sure process of her awakening to what this man, who "has no good
red blood in his body," really is—a cold, shallow pedant, whose
entire existence is bound up in researches, with regard to which he
even shrinks from inquiry as to whether all he has for years been
vaguely attempting has not been anticipated, and whose intense
and absorbing egoism makes the remotest hint of depreciation
pierce like a dagger. The first faint dawn of discovery breaks on her

almost immediately on their arrival at Rome. Conscious of her want of mere fsthetic culture—neglected in the past as a turning aside from life's highest aims—she has looked forward to his guidance and support for the supply of this want as enlarging her whole being; broadening and deepening, refining and elevating all its sympathies. For all shadow of aid or sympathy here, she finds herself as utterly alone as if she were in a trackless and uninhabited desert. Nay, more: he who sits by her side is as cold and dead to all sensations or emotions that art can enkindle, as the glorious marbles amid which they wander. Soon she finds herself relegated to the society and fellowship of her maid; her husband is less to her, is incapable p. 83of being other than less, amid those transcendant treasures of architecture, painting, and sculpture, than a hired guide or cicerone would be.

Soon follows the scene where her timid offer of humble service is thrown back with all the irritation of that absorbing egoism which is the very essence and life-in-death of the man. For the first and only time, a faint cry of conscious irritation escapes her, followed by an anguish of repentance so deep, so meekly, humbly self-accusing, it reveals to us more of her truest and innermost life than pages of elaborate description could do. A single sentence descriptive of her mood even in that first irritation brings before us her deepest soul, and the utter absence of self isolation and self-insistence there:— "However just her indignation might be, her ideal was not *to claim justice*, but *to give tenderness.*"

She meets Ladislaw; and he more than hints to her that the dim, vague labours and accumulations of years which have constituted her husband's nearest approach to life have been labour in vain; that the "great mind" has been toiling, with feeble uncertain steps, in a path which has already been trodden into firmness and completeness; toiling in wilful and obdurate ignorance that other and abler natures have more than anticipated all he has been painfully and abortively labouring to accomplish. Again a cry bursts from the wounded heart, seemingly of anger against her informant, really of anguish—p. 84anguish, not for her own sinking hopes, but for the burden of disappointment and failure which she instinctively perceives must, sooner or later, fall on the husband who is thus throwing away life in vain.

So it goes on, through all the ever-darkening problem of her married, yet unmated, life. Effort, always more earnest on the part of her yearning, unselfish tenderness, to establish true relations between them; to find in him something of that sweet support, that expansive and elevating force, silently entering into her own innermost life, which her first childlike trust inspired; to become to him, even if no more may be, that to which her childlike humility at first alone aspired—eyes to his weakness, and strength and freedom to his pen. So it goes on; ever-gnawing pain and anguish, as all her yearning love and pity is thrown back, and that dulled insensate heart and all-absorbing egoism can find only irritation in her timid attempts at sympathy, only dread of detection of the half-conscious futility of all his labours, in her humble proffers of even mechanical aid. Not easily can even the most fervid and penetrative imagination conceive what, to a nature like Dorothea's, such a life must be, with its never-ceasing, ever-gathering pain; its longing tenderness not even actively repelled, but simply ignored or misinterpreted; its humblest, equally with its highest yearnings, baffled and shattered against that triple mail of shallowest self-includedness. And all has to be borne in silence and p. 85alone. No word, no look, no sign, betrays to other eye the inward anguish, the deepening disappointment, the slow dying away of hope. Nay, for long, on indeed to the bitter close, failure seems to her to be almost wholly on her own side; and repentance and self-upbraiding leave no room for resentment.

Ere long—indeed, very soon—another, and, if possible, a still deeper humiliation comes upon her,—another, and, in some respects, a keener pang, as showing more intensely how entirely she stands alone, is thrown into her life,—in her husband's jealousy of Ladislaw. Yet jealousy it cannot be called. Of any emotion so comparatively profound, any passion so comparatively elevated, that self-absorbed, self-tormenting nature is utterly incapable. Jealousy, in some degree, presupposes love; love not wholly absorbed in self, but capable to some extent of going forth from our own mean and sordid self-inclusion in sympathetic relation, dependence, and aid, towards another existence. In Mr Casaubon there is no capability, no possibility of this. What in him wears the aspect of jealousy is simply and solely self-love, callous irritation, that any one should—

not stand above, but—approach himself in importance with the woman he has purchased as a kind of superior slave. For long her guileless innocence and purity, her utter inability to conceive such a feeling, leaves her only in doubt and perplexity before it; long after it has first betrayed itself, she reveals this incapability in the fullest extent, and in the way most p. 86intensely irritating to her husband's self-love—by her simple-hearted proposal that whatever of his property would devolve on her should be shared with Ladislaw. Then it is that Casaubon is roused to inflict on her the last long and bitter anguish; to lay on her for life—had not death intervened—the cold, soul-benumbing, life contracting clutch of "the Dead Hand." In the innocence of her entire relations with Ladislaw, not the faintest dawning of thought connects itself with him in her husband's cold, insistent demand on her blind obedience to his will. She thinks alone of his thus binding her to a lifelong task, not only hard and ungenial, but one that shall absorb and fetter all her energies, restrain all her faculties, impair and frustrate all her higher and broader aims, make impossible all that better and purer fulness of life for which she yearns. Then follows the long and painful struggle,—a struggle so agonising to such a nature, that only one nearly akin to her own can adequately conceive or picture it. For it is a struggle not primarily to forego any certain or fancied mere personal good. On one side is ranged tenderest pitifulness over her husband's wasted life and energies, even though she knows those energies have been wasted—that life has been thrown away—on an object in which there is no gain to humanity, no advancement of human well-being, no profit even to himself, save, perchance, a barren and useless notoriety at last; an object that has been already far more fully and ably achieved. p. 87On the other stands her clear undoubting *conscience* of her own truest and highest course,—the course to which every prompting of the Divine within impels her,—that she shall not thus isolate herself within this narrowest sphere, shut herself out from all social sympathies and social outgoings, and sacrifice to the Dead Hand that holds her in its cold remorseless clutch every interest that may be intrusted to her. We instinctively shudder at the result; but we never doubt what the answer will be. We know that the tender, womanly, wifely pitifulness, the causeless remorse, will be the nearest and most urgent conscience, and will prevail. The agonised assent is to be given; but it falls on the ear of the dead.

It is scarcely necessary to follow Dorothea minutely through all the details of her widowed relations to Mr Casaubon. Enough that these are all in touching and beautiful harmony with everything that has gone before. No resentment, no recalcitration against all the ever-gathering perplexity, pain, and anguish he has caused her—nothing but the sweet unfailing pitifulness, the uncalled-for repentance, almost remorse, over her own assumed shortcomings and deficiencies—her failures to be to him what in those first days of her childlike simplicity and innocence she had hoped she might become. Even on the discovery of the worse than treachery, of the mean insulting malignity with which, trusting to her confiding purity and truthfulness, he had sought to grasp her for life in p. 88his "Dead Hand" with regard to Ladislaw, and she only escaped the irrevocable bond her own blindly-given pledge would have fixed around her by his death,—the momentary and violent shock of revulsion from her dead husband, who had had hidden thoughts of her, perhaps perverting everything she said or did, *terrified her as if it had been a sin.*

It is not alone, however, toward her husband that this simple, unconscious self-devotion and self-abnegation of Dorothea Brooke displays itself. Toward every one with whom she comes in contact, it steals out unobtrusively and silently, as the dew from heaven on the tender grass, to each and all according to the kind and nearness of that relation. Even for her "pulpy" uncle she has no supercilious contempt—no sense of isolation or separation; not even the consciousness of toleration toward him. Toward Celia, with her delicious commonplace of rather superficial yet *naove* worldly wisdom, her half-conscious selfishness, her baby-worship, and her inimitable "staccato," she is more than tolerant. She looks up to her as in many respects a superior, even though her own far higher instincts and aims of life cannot accept her as an aid and guidance toward the realisation of these. Even at old Featherstone's funeral, her one emotion is of pitiful sorrow over that loveless mockery of all human pity and love; and for the "Frog-faced" there is no feeling but sympathetic compassion for his apparent loneliness amongst strangers, who all stand p. 89aloof and look askance on him. Into all Lydgate's plans, into the whole question of the hospital and all he hopes to achieve through means of it, she throws herself with swift intelligence, with active, eager sympathy, as a probable instrumentality by which at least one phase of suffering may be redressed or allayed. And in the hour of his deep humiliation, when all others have fallen away from his side, when the wife of his bosom forsakes him in callous and heartless resentment of what was done for her sake alone; when he stands out the mark of scorn and obloquy for all save Farebrother, and scans and all but loathes himself—she, with her artless trust in the best of humanity, in the strength of her instinctive recognition of the merest glimmering of whatever is true and right and high in others, comes to his side, yields him at once her fullest confidence, gives him with frank simplicity her aid, and enables him, so far as determined prejudice and uncharity will allow, to right himself before others.

Reference has already been made to her whole relations, from first to last, with Ladislaw. It is not easy to conceive anything more touchingly beautiful than these, more perfectly in harmony with her whole nature. Of anything approaching either coquetry or prudery she is incapable. The utter absence of all self-consciousness, whether of external beauty or inward loveliness; the ethereal purity, the childlike trustfulness, the instinctive recognition of all that is p. 90true and earnest and high in Ladislaw, through all the surface appearance of indecision, of vague uncertain aim and purpose and limited object in life; no thought of what is ordinarily called love toward him, of love on his part toward her—ever dawns upon her guileless innocence. Through all her yearning to do justice to him as regards the property of her dead husband, which she looks upon as fairly and justly his, or at least to be shared with him, there arises before her the determination of her dead husband that it should not be so; and her sweet regretful pitifulness over that meagre wasted life prevails. Anon, when at last through the will she is made aware of the crowning act of that concentrated callousness of heart and soul, and of the true nature of the benumbing grasp it had sought to lay on her for life, and had so far succeeded in doing, then for the first time her "tremulous" maiden purity and simplicity awakens, and for the first time it enters her mind that Ladislaw could, under any circumstances, become her lover; that another had thought of them in that light, and that he himself had been conscious of such a possibility arising. The later scenes between them are characterised by a quiet beauty, a suppressed power and pathos, compared to which most other love-scenes in fiction appear dull and coarse. The tremulous yearning of her love, as it awakens more and more to distinct consciousness within; the new-born shyness blent with the old, trustful, frank simplicity,—bring before us a picture p. 91of love, in its purest and most beautiful aspect, such as cannot easily be paralleled in fiction.

Toward her late husband's parishioners there is the same wise instinctive insight as to their true needs, the same thoughtful and provident consideration that characterises her in every relation into which she is brought. If she at once objects, on their behoof, to Mr Tyke's so-called "apostolic" preaching, it is that she means by that, sermons about "imputed righteousness and the prophecies in the Apocalypse. I have always been thinking of the different ways in which Christianity is taught, and whenever I find one way that makes it a wider blessing than any other, I cling to that as the truest—I mean that which takes in the most good of all kinds, and brings in the most people as sharers in it." And in her final selection of Mr Farebrother, she is guided not alone by her sense of his general and essential fitness for the work assigned to him, but also in some degree by her desire to make whist-playing for money, and the comparatively inferior society into which it necessarily draws him, no longer a need of his outer life.

Of all the less prominent relations into which Dorothea Brooke is brought, there is not one more touchingly tender, or in which her whole nature is drawn more beautifully out, than that to Rose Vincy. Between these two, at least on the side of the hard unpenetrable incarnation of self-inclusion and self-pleasing, any approach to harmony or sympathy is p. 92impossible. There is not even any true ground of womanhood on which Rosamond can meet Dorothea; for she is nearly as far removed from womanhood as Tito Melema is from manliness or manhood. Yet even here the tender pitifulness of Dorothea overpasses a barrier that to any other would be impassable. In her sweet, instinctive, universal sympathy for human sorrow and pain, she finds a common ground of union; and in no fancied sense of superiority—solely from the sense of common human need — she strives to console, to elevate, to lead back to hope and trust, with a gentle yet steadfast simplicity all her own.

Such, as portrayed by unquestionably the greatest fictionist of the time — is it too much to say, the greatest genius of our English nineteenth century? — is the nineteenth century St Theresa.

The question may be raised by some of George Eliot's readers whether it constitutes the best and completest ethical teaching that fiction can attain, to bring before its readers such high ideals of the possibilities of humanity — of the aim and purpose of life toward which it should ever aspire. Were the author's canvas occupied with such portraitures alone — with Romolas and Fedalmas, Dinah Morrises and Dorothea Brookes, Daniel Derondas and Adam Bedes, even Mr Tryans and Mr Gilfils — the question might call for full discussion, and a contrast might be unfavourably drawn between the author and him whose p. 93emphatic praise it is that he "holds the mirror up to nature." But the great artist for all time brings before us not only an Iago and an Edmund, an Angelo and an Iachimo, a Regan and a Goneril, but a Miranda and an Imogen, an Isabella and a Viola, a Cordelia and a Desdemona, with every conceivable intermediate shade of human character and life; and in George Eliot we have the same clearly-defined contrasts and endless variety. That a Becky Sharp and a Beatrix Castlewood are drawn with the consummate skill and force of the most perfect artist in his own special sphere our age has produced, few will be disposed to deny: and that they have momentous lessons to teach us all, — that they may by sheer antagonism rouse some from dreams of selfish vanity and corruption, and awaken within some germ of better and purer elements of life, — will scarcely be disputed. But it is not from these, or such as these, that the highest and noblest, the purest and most penetrative, the most extended and enduring teaching and elevation of the world has come. That has come emphatically from Him whose self-chosen name, "the Son of Man," designates Him the ideal of humanity on earth; Him who is at once the "Lamb of God" and "the Lion of the tribe of Judah," the "Good Shepherd," and the stern and fearless but ever-righteous Judge — the concentration of all tender and holy love, and of divinest scorn of, and revulsion from, everything mean and false in humanity; Him who for p. 94the repentant sinner has no harsher word of rebuke than "Go and sin no more," and who over the self-righteous, self-wrapt, all-despising Pharisees thundered back, to His own ultimate destruction, His terrible "Woe unto you *hypocrites.*" He too stands out, not isolated or severed, but prominent, amid every conceivable phase and gradation of human character, from a John to a Judas; touches each and all at some point of living contact; meets them with tender sympathy, with gentle patience, and pitying love, over their weaknesses and falls. Can the true artist err in aiming, according to his nature or to the purity and elevation of his genius, to approach in his portraitures such ideals as this great typical exemplar of our humanity, whose influence has for eighteen centuries been stealing down into the hearts and souls of men to elevate and refine, and who is now, and who is more and more becoming, the paramount factor in individual character, and in social and political relations? Or can such ideals, presented before us, fail to arouse in some degree the better elements of our humanity, and to lead us to strive toward the realisation of these?

In wonderfully drawn and finished yet never obtruded contrast to this beautiful creation comes before us Rosamond Vincy. Outwardly even more characterised by every personal charm, save that one living and crowning charm which outshines from the soul within; to the eye, therefore — such eyes as can p. 95penetrate no deeper than the surface — prettier, more graceful, more accomplished and fascinating, than Dorothea Brooke; — it is difficult to conceive a more utterly unlovable example of womanhood, whether as maiden or wife. Hard and callous of heart and dead of soul, incapable of one thought or emotion that rises above or extends beyond self, insistent on her own petty claims and ambitions to the exclusion of all others, ever aiming to achieve these, now by dogged sullen persistence, now by mean concealments and frauds, no more repellent portraiture of womanhood has ever been placed before us. The fundamental character of her entire home relations is, on her first appearance, drawn by a single delicate touch — her objecting to her brother's red herring, or rather to its presence after she enters the room, because its odour jars on her sense of pseudo-refinement. In her relation to her husband there is not from first to last one shadow of anything that can be called love, no approach to sympathy or harmony of life. She looks on him solely as a means for removing herself to what she considers a higher social circle, securing to her greater ease, freedom, and luxury of daily life, and ultimately withdrawing her to a wider sphere of petty and selfish enjoyment. Seeking these ends, she resorts to every mean device of deceit and concealment. Utterly callous and impenetrable to his feelings, to every manlier instinct within him, as she is utterly insensible of, and indeed incapable of, p. 96entering into his higher and wider professional aims, she not only ignores these, but in her dull and hard insensibility runs counter to, and tramples on them all.

Even toward Mary Garth there is nothing approaching true friendship or affection; no power of recognising her honesty, unselfishness, and earnestness of nature. She is nothing to her but a tool and *confidante*, the recipient of her own petty hopes and desires, worries and cares.

All Dorothea's gentle, unobtrusive attempts to soothe, to win her back to truer and better relations with her husband, and to awaken to active life and exercise the true womanhood, which she in her sweet instinct believes to be inherent in all her sex, are met by hard indifference or dull resistance. And in the one act of apparent friendliness or rather explanation toward Dorothea, she is actuated far less by sympathy or desire to clear away what has come between her and Ladislaw, than by sullen resentment against the latter for his rejection of her unseemly and unwifely advances to him.

In the position she at last takes up toward Ladislaw, there is no approach to anything in the very least resembling love—even illicit and overmastering passion. Of that her very nature is incapable. She is influenced solely by resentment against her husband, and his failure to fulfil her vain and self-absorbed dreams; by the hope that he will remove her to a sphere which will give wider scope to her heartless p. 97selfishness, and take her away from the social disappointments and humiliations into which that selfishness has mainly plunged her. In every relation of life near or far, important or trivial, amid all environments, under all impulsion toward anything purer and better, Rosamond Vincy is ever the same; as consistent and unvarying in her hard unwomanliness and impenetrable, insistent self-seeking, as is Dorothea in every opposite characteristic. And even while the picture in one way fascinates the reader, it is the fascination of ever-increasing contempt and loathing where the extremest charity can hardly even pity; and from it we ever turn to that of St Theresa with the more intense refreshment alike of mind and heart, and the deeper sense of its elevating and refining influence.

Among the many clearly defined and vividly drawn portraits in this great work, it would be easy, did space permit, to select others well worthy of detailed examination, and illustrative of the salient aim and tendency of all George Eliot's works. The homely yet beautiful family groups of the Garths, Celia and Sir James Chettam, the Bulstrodes, {97} even p. 98the wretched old Featherstone, and the crowd of vultures "waiting for death around him," all more or less illustrate the fundamental principle of the highest ethics—that self-abnegation is life, elevation, purity, uplifting our humanity toward the Divine; that self-seeking and self-isolation tend surely toward moral and spiritual death. Two, however, stand out so delicately yet clearly defined and contrasting, that they claim brief consideration before passing from this great work—Lydgate and Farebrother.

The whole character and career of Lydgate are brought before us with the skill of the consummate artist. At first he appears as a man of massive and energetic proportions, of high professional impulses and aims, resolute to carry these through against all difficulty and amid all indifference and opposition, and apparently seeking through these aims the general good of humanity—the alleviation of suffering, and the arrestment, it may be, of death. But even then there are signs of inherent weakness, and all but certain decline and fall. There are indications of arrogant self sufficiency and supercilious contempt for others; of undue deference for Bulstrode, not from respect or esteem, but as a tool to further his views; and a tendency to treat patients not as human beings but as cases—objects to experiment on, and verify hypotheses regarding pathology and disease, all which betray a nature not attuned to the highest and noblest pitch, and that cannot be expected to stand in the p. 99hour of trial. His first direct lapse is when, against his secret conviction, he supports Tyke as hospital chaplain in opposition to Farebrother; but mainly in mere defiance and resentment of the general style of his reception at the Board meeting, and the opposition he encounters there. Anon comes his marriage to Rosamond Vincy,—a marriage prompted by no true affection, but solely by the fascination of her prettiness, her external grace and accomplishments. Led on mainly by his own taste for luxury and external show, he plunges into extravagances of every kind. Debt inevitably follows, crippling his resources, cramping his energies, fettering him as regards all his higher professional aims and efforts. To his wife he looks in vain for sympathy or aid. She only aggravates the difficulties and harassments of his life by her callous selfishness, her dull obdurate insistance on all her own claims, her mean deceits and concealments. Embarrassments of every kind thicken around him; and at last in the all but universal estimation of his fellows, and nearly in his own, in the hope of temporary relief he becomes accessory to murder. His end is as sad a one for his character, and in his circumstances, as can well be conceived: falling from all his high if somewhat arrogant professional aims, his hopes of elevating the general practitioner, and of raising medicine from an art to a science, into the fashionable London lady's doctor.

Though Mr Farebrother occupies a somewhat less p. 100prominent place in the narrative, he is delineated with not less consummate skill. He comes before us at first a man of genial kindly sympathies, frankly alive to, and frankly acknowledging, his own deficiencies. There is an utter absence of pretence and affectation about him, a graceful and engaging simplicity and frankness of whole nature, that can hardly fail to win the heart. All his home relations—toward mother and sisters—are singularly touching. Feeling all his defects as a clergyman, half laughing, half apologetic over his devotion to his favourite Coleoptera, and admitting that which is so far a necessity to him, not of choice, but of actual external need in his narrow circumstances—admitting, too, the comparatively inferior and uncongenial society into which he is drawn—the full revelation of his nobler and higher nature begins. His true and deep appreciation of Mary Garth, and tender, devoted, and unselfish love for her, more clearly reveal his innate manliness, self-denial, and simplicity of character. This revelation is still further unfolded before us in his entire relations with Fred Vincy. That firm persistent interview in the billiard-room, is actuated by the one absorbing and self-abnegating desire that he may still be saved from the moral and spiritual decay impending over him: and when, in answer to Fred's appeal for his intercession, we discover the blighting of his own hopes, the shattering of his love, the tender heart stricken to the core should Fred prove, as he p. 101suspects, his successful rival, we discern in him a nature of the finest capabilities, and surely tending on and up toward the noblest ends; and we part from him as from a dear and valued friend, whose society has cheered and elevated us, whose pure simplicity of nature has refuted our vain pretensions, and whose memory clings to us as a fragrance and refreshment.

There now only remains the last yet published, and in the estimation of many, the greatest, of George Eliot's works — 'Daniel Deronda.' In it the author takes up — not a new scope, but extends one that has all along been present, and that indeed was inevitably associated with her great ethical principle, — the bringing of that principle definitely and directly to bear upon not only every domestic but every social and political relation of human life. This tendency may be briefly expressed in the old and profound words: "No man liveth to himself; no man dieth to himself." As we aim toward the true and good and pure, or surrender ourselves the slaves of self and sense, we live or die to God or to the devil.

Before, however, proceeding to detailed examination of this remarkable work, it seems necessary to draw attention to one objection which has been urged against it — the prominent introduction of the Jewish element into its scheme. Such objection could scarcely have been put forward by any one who considers what the Jew has been in the past — what an enormous factor p. 102his past and present have been and are, in the development and progress of our highest civilisation. Historically, we first meet him coming forth from the Arabian desert, a rude unlettered herdsman, in intelligence, cultivation, and morality far below the tribes among whom he is thrown. A terrible weapon arms him — a theism stern, hard, and pitiless, beyond, perhaps, all the world has ever seen. To the bravest and best of his race — a Moses and a Joshua, a Deborah and a Jephtha — this presents ruthless massacre, the vilest treachery, offering up a sacrifice the dearest and most loved, not as mere permissible acts, but as deeds of religious homage solemnly enjoined by his Most High. This theism has one central thought in which it practically stands alone, and which it was the aim of all its supposed heads and legislators to keep inviolate amid all surrounding antagonisms—the intense assertion of the Divine unity. "Hear, O Israel! the Lord thy God is *one* Lord." In these brief words lies the very core of Judaism. So long as he holds fast by this central truth, the Jew is exhibited to us as practically omnipotent. Seas and floods divide before him; hosts numberless as the sands are scattered at his appearance; cyclopean walls fall prone at his trumpet-blast.

And this thought of the Divine unity, thus intensely pervading the national life, upfolds within capacity of indefinite development. No long time in the life of a nation elapses ere "The Lord thy God is a p. 103jealous God, visiting the iniquity of the fathers upon the children," became "As a father pitieth his children, so the Lord pitieth them that fear Him." "Can a woman forget her sucking child, that she should not have compassion on the son of her womb? Yea, she *may* forget; yet will not *I* forget thee."

In no sense of the word was the Jew a creature of imagination. The stern and hard realities of his life would seem to have crushed out every trace of the fsthetic element within him. Yet from among these people arose a literature, especially a hymnology, which has never been approached elsewhere; and it arose emphatically and distinctly out of the great central and animating thought of the Divine unity. To the Psalms so-called of David, the glorious outbursts of sacred song in their mythico-historical books, as in Isaiah {103} and some of the minor prophets, the finest of the Vedic or Orphic hymns or the Homeric ballads are cold and spiritless. These address themselves to scholars alone, or chiefly to a cultivated few, and address themselves to them eloquently and gloriously. The hymns of the Jews have so interpenetrated the very heart of humanity, p. 104so identified themselves with the best longings, the noblest aspirations, the purest hopes, and the deepest sorrows of man, that still, after more than twenty centuries, that wonderful hymnology breathes up day after day, week after week, from millions of households and hearts. They outbreathe its fervid aspirations toward a purer and diviner life. They give expression to its profound wailings over degradation and fall. They give utterance on all the inscrutable mysteries of existence; and ever and anon as the clouds and darkness break away from the Infinite Love,—they burst forth into the exultant cry, "God reigneth, let the earth be glad. . . . Give thanks at remembrance of His *holiness.*"

But important as is this factor of Judaism, there is another generally considered which has perhaps exercised a still more profound and cumulative influence on the civilisation especially of the West. This lies in the intense indestructible nationality of the race. Eighteen centuries have passed since they became a people, "scattered and peeled," their "holy and beautiful house" a ruin, their capital a desolation, their land proscribed to the exile's foot. During these centuries deluge after deluge of so-called barbarians has swept over Asia and Europe: Hun and Tartar, Alan and Goth, Suev and Vandal,—we attach certain vague meanings to the names, but can the most learned scholar identify one individual of the true unmingled blood? All have disappeared, merged in p. 105the race they overran, in the kingdoms they conquered and devastated. The Jew alone, through these centuries, has remained the Jew: proscribed, persecuted, hunted as never was tiger or wolf, he is as vividly defined, as unchangeably national, as when he stood alone, everywhere without and beyond the despised and hated Gentile. And this intense and conservative nationality springs essentially out of the central conception of Judaism, "God is *one.*" Be He the incarnation of pitiless vengeance, hardening Pharaoh's heart that He may execute sevenfold wrath on him and his people; be He the Good Shepherd, who "gathers the lambs in His arms," and for their sakes "tempers His rough wind in the day of His east wind;"—to the Jew He has been and is, "I am the Lord; that is My name; and My glory will I not give to another."

Through those long ages of darkness, devil-worship, and polytheism (in its grossest forms all around), the Jew stood up in unfaltering protest against all. Persecutions, proscriptions, tortures in every form, were of no avail. On the gibbet, on the rack, amid the flames, his last words embodied the central confession of Judaism, "O Israel, the Lord *thy* God is one Lord." Christianity, the appointed custodier of the still more central truth, "God is love," had to all appearance failed of its mission; had not only merged its higher message in a theistic presentation, dark and terroristic as that of Judaism at its dawn, but had absorbed into p. 106its scheme, under other names, the gods many who swarm all around it; till nowhere and never, save by some soul upborne by its own fervour above these dense fogs and mists, could individual man meet his God face to face, and realise that higher life of the soul which is His free gift to all who seek it. Between this heathenised Christianity and Judaism, the contrast was the sharpest, the contest the most embittered and unvarying. Elsewhere we hear of times of toleration and indulgence even for the hunted Monotheist, — in medieval Christendom, never. The Inquisition plied its rack for the Jews with a more fiendish zeal than even for the hated Morisco. The mob held him responsible for plague and famine; and kings and nobles hounded the mob on to indiscriminate massacre. The Jew lived on through it all, — lived, multiplied, and prospered, and became more and more emphatically the Jew. Is it too much to say that in the West in particular, where this contrast and contest were keenest, Judaism was, during these long ages of terror and darkness, the great conservator of the vital truth of the Divine unity, under whatever forms science or philosophy may now attempt to define this; and in being so, became the conservator of that thought, without the vivifying power of which, howsoever imperfectly apprehended, all human advance is impossible? Is it exaggerating the importance of the Jew and his intense nationality, based on such a truth, to say that, but for his presence, "scattered and p. 107peeled," among all nations, the Europe we now know could not have been? And this indestructible nationality, for whose existence miracle has been called into account — has it no significance in the future equal to what it has had in the past? There seems an impression that the Jew is being absorbed by other races. We hear much of relaxing Judaisms; of rituals and beliefs assimilating to those around them; of peculiarities being laid aside, that have withstood the wear and tear of centuries. The inference is sought to be drawn that the Jew is beginning to feel his isolation, and to sink his own national life amid that among which he dwells. We accept all the facts; but can only see in them that, under the influence of the profound thought and research of its great leaders, Judaism is shaking off the dust of ages, and is more vividly awaking to its mission upon earth. We believe it is coming forth from all this superficial change, more intensely and powerfully Judaical, more penetrated and vivified by that thought which for untold centuries has been the life of its life. What is to be its specific future as a leader in the advancement and redemption of humanity, none can foresee. But it seems the reverse of strange that a genius like George Eliot's should have been powerfully attracted by this problem; and that, in one of her noblest works, she should have very prominently addressed herself to at least a partial solution of it. That the solution she suggests is a noble one, few who carefully consider p. 108the subject will, we think, deny. The establishment of a Jewish polity, in the true sense of the word a theocracy, where the Infinite Holiness is supreme, and in its supremacy is included a reign of justice, purity, and love;—the establishment of such a polity locally between the materialistic proclivities of the West and the psychological subtleties of the East, mediative between them, communicating from each to each of those essentials to human life in which the other is deficient, is a conception worthy of her genius.

Another minor and very trivial objection to the presence of this Jewish element need be no more than adverted to. It is the presence of such different types as the mean-souled scoundrel Lapidoth; the shrewd self-approving trader Cohen, with the inimitable picture of a home-life so pleasant and kindly; the vague intense enthusiasm, the ardent aspirations and fervent hopes of Mordecai; the absorbing Judaism of the Physician; the fierce revulsion of his daughter against her race and name; the meek, delicate, ethereal purity of Mirah; the innate Jewish yearnings and aspirations of Deronda, expanded by all the breadth that could be given by the highest Anglo-Saxon culture and training. To those who take exception to this, it is answer more than sufficient that, as an artist, it was necessary to present every typical phase of Jewish character and life; and we confess there are other passages in the work we could better spare than p. 109these delicious pictures of a London-Jewish pawnbroker at home.

Of all the characters portrayed in fiction, there is perhaps not one so difficult to analyse and define as that which stands out so prominently in this wonderful work, Gwendolen Harleth. At once attractive and repellent—fascinating in no ordinary degree, and yet, in the estimation of all around her, hard, cold, and worldly-minded—bewitching, alike from her beauty, grace, and accomplishments, yet a superficial and seemingly heartless coquette,—she presents a combination of at once some of the finest and some of the meanest qualities of woman. Her hardness towards her fond, doting mother, and her contempt for her sisters, are conspicuous almost from her first appearance. Her arrogant defiance of Deronda in the gambling-house, and the fierce revulsion of pride with which she received the return of her necklace, are entirely in keeping with these characteristics. And the news of the reduction of her family to utter poverty awakens no emotion save on her own behalf alone. Yet, ever and anon, faint gleams of tenderness towards her gentle mother break forth, though soon obscured by the bitter insistance with which her own claims to station, wealth, and luxury assert themselves. Her first acceptance of Grandcourt represents this phase of her twofold nature; her rejection of him and flight from him, after her interview with Mrs Glasher, are equally characteristic of the second. That rejection p. 110is actuated much more by resentment against Mrs Glasher, that she should have dared to anticipate her in anything resembling affection he had to give, and against him, that he should have presumed to offer to her a heart already sealed to anything resembling love, than by the faintest approach to it in her own. The leap, as it were, by which she ultimately accepts him, is merely a quick, half-conscious instinct to secure her own deliverance from poverty, and the attainment of those higher external enjoyments of life for which she conceived herself formed; and if, in addition, a thought of relieving the wants of her mother and sisters obtrudes, it holds only a very secondary place in her mind. Deeming herself born for dominion over every male heart, in her utter childish ignorance of human character, she deems that Grandcourt also shall be her slave.

But through all her relations with that magnificent incarnation of self-isolation and self-love, she is compelled to cower before him. Again and again she attempts to turn, only to be crushed under his heel as ruthlessly as a worm. During the yachting voyage it is the same; intense inward revulsion on the one side—cold, inexorable despotism on the other.

The drowning scene first begins to stir the better nature within her. The intensity of terror with which she regards the involuntary murderous thought, and which prompted her leap into the water, the fervour of remorse which followed, all begin to indicate a p. 111nature which may yet be attuned to the highest qualities. On the other hand, the sweet clinging trust with which she hangs on

Deronda, looks up to him, feels that for her every possibility of good lies in association with him, are those of a guileless, artless child. She has been called a hard-hearted, callous woman of the world: her worldliness is on the surface alone. Her first cry to Deronda is the piteous wail of a forsaken child; the letter with which their relations close is the fond yearning of a child towards one whom she looks up to as protector and saviour.

Grandcourt is portrayed before us in more massive and simple proportions as a type of concentrated selfishness. We dare not despise him, we cannot loathe him—we stand bowed and awe-stricken before him. He never for a moment falls from that calm dignity of pride and self-isolation—never for a moment softens into respect for anything without himself. Without a moment's exception he is ever consistent, imperturbable in his self-containedness, ruthlessly crushing all things from dog to wife, under his calm, cold, slighting contempt. He stands up before us, not so much indomitable as simply unassailable. We cannot conceive the boldest approaching or encroaching on him—all equally shiver and quail before that embodiment of the devil as represented by human self-love.

Fain would we linger over the Jewish girl, Mirah. She has been spoken of as characterless; to us it seems as if few characters of more exquisite loveliness p. 112have ever been portrayed. From her first appearance robed in her meek despair, through all her subsequent relations with Deronda, her brother, and Gwendolen, there is the same delicate purity, the same tender meekness, the same full acceptance of the life of a Jewess as—in harmony with the life of her race—one of "sufferance." Even as her spirits gladden in that sunny Meyrick home, with its delicious interiors, and brighten under the noble-hearted musician Klesmer's encouragement, the brightness refers to something entirely without herself. In one sense far more acquainted with the evil that is in the world than Gwendolen with all her alleged worldliness, it is her shrinking from the least approach to this that prompts her strange, apparently hopeless flight in search of the mother she had loved so dearly. Her sad, humble complaints that she has not been a good Jewess, because she has been inevitably cut off from the use of Jewish books, and restrained by her scoundrel father from attendance at Jewish worship, find their answer in her deep unfailing sense of her share in the national doom of suffering. We feel with Mrs Meyrick "that she is a pearl, and the mud has only washed her." In her startling interview with Gwendolen, the sudden indignant protest which the inquiry of the latter calls out is a protest against even a hint of evil being directed towards that which has been best and highest to her. Her love for Deronda steals into the maiden purity of her soul with an unconscious p. 113delicacy which cannot be surpassed; and as she parts from us by his side, we feel that she is no Judith or Esther, but the meek Mary of the annunciation, going forth on her unknown mission of love with the words, "Behold the handmaid of the Lord."

Beside the exquisitely meek child-figure, with the small delicate head faintly drooping under the sorrow which is the heritage of her race, stands up Deronda in his calm dignity. As he lies on the grass, and the first faint glimmering of the possible origin of his life breaks upon him, even the first inevitable risings of resentment against Sir Hugo are softened and toned down by the old yearning affection; and the longings for the unknown mother, intense as they are, yet shrink from full discovery of what she may have been or may still be. He and he alone, in unconscious dignity, stands up uncowering before Grandcourt. His whole relations to Mordecai are characterised by a deep suppressed enthusiasm, that fully responds to the enthusiast's soul. Towards Gwendolen every word he speaks, every act he does, is marked by the fervour of his whole nature; but it is beside the fair head drooping under its burden of hereditary sorrow that Deronda passes from our sight, the fitting type of him who shall yet, sooner or later, re-establish that great Jewish theocracy so long dreamt of, and reaffirm that Judaism yet holds a great place in human life and civilisation.

We have throughout had no intention of dealing p. 114with George Eliot merely as the artist; but if we have succeeded in showing this unity of moral purpose and aim as pervading all her works, as giving rise to their variety by reason of the varieties and modifications it necessitates in order to its full illustration, and as ministered to, directly or indirectly, by all the accessory characters and incidents of these creations,—the question naturally arises, whether this does not constitute her an artist of the highest possible order.

But the true worth of George Eliot's works rests, we think, on higher grounds than any mere perfection of artistic finish; on this ground, specially, that among all our fictionists she stands out as the deepest, broadest, and most catholic illustrator of the true ethics of Christianity; the most earnest and persistent expositor of the true doctrine of the Cross, that we are born and should live to something higher than the love of happiness; the most subtle and profound commentator on the solemn words, "He that loveth his soul shall lose it: he that hateth his soul shall keep it unto life eternal."

Footnotes:

{15} The translators of our English Bible, possibly perplexed by the seeming paradox involved in these remarkable words, have taken an unwarrantable freedom with the original, in rendering the Greek ψυχη, invariably the synonym of the soul, the spiritual and undying element in man, by "life" — the ζωη of all Greek literature so-called, sacred and profane alike; the synonym of that life which is his in common with the beast of the field and the tree of the forest.

{29} Perhaps no finer and more subtle illustration of this "instinct of the gentleman" can be found in literature than when, at the moment of Harold Transome's deepest humiliation, where Jermyn claims him as his son, good old Sir Marmaduke, not only his political opponent but personally disliking him, for the first and only time in all their intercourse addresses him by his Christian name, "Come, *Harold*."

{97} In connection with Bulstrode occurs one of those delicate indications of character, condensed into a few words, which others would expand into pages, peculiar to George Eliot. It occurs in the depth of his humiliation, when his wife, hitherto comparatively characterless, in full token of her acceptance of their fallen lot, "takes off all her ornaments, and puts on a plain gown, and instead of wearing her much adorned-cap and large bows of hair, brushes down her hair, and puts on a plain bonnet-cap, which makes her look like an early Methodist."

{103} Does all poetry ancient or modern, so-called sacred or profane, contain an image more impressive and majestic than that in the "doom of Babylon," as the great incarnation of pride and luxury descends to its place: "Hades from beneath is moved for thee to meet thee at thy coming: it stirreth up the dead for thee, even all the chief ones of the earth; it hath raised up from their thrones all the kings of the nations."